KILL ME A HUSBAND

Alma was breathing quickly, the way she did sometimes when they made love. Grasping Ward's arm, she shoved him through the door, her eyes shining with a strange brilliance.

Her husband was there on the bed, relaxed in sleep and unaware of danger.

"Now!" she whispered hoarsely.

Ward grasped the sash weight in both hands, his slender body quaking with tension. A tortured moan escaped his lips. He had to do what Alma wanted or he'd lose her forever. And the very thought of never again possessing her eager, passion-hungry body impelled him to lift the sash weight high in the air.

"Now!" screamed Alma with frantic urgency. "Do it now!"

AUTHOR'S PROFILE

Tedd Thomey was born in Butte, Montana in 1920 and is a graduate of the University of California. He served in the Marine Corps as a second lieutenant during World War II.

After his war stint he became a reporter and feature writer on the San Diego UNION-TRIBUNE and the San Francisco CHRONICLE and he is currently a columnist and telegraph editor on the Long Beach INDEPENDENT-PRESS-TELEGRAM.

He has been a professional free lance writer for 12 years and his magazine stories and articles have appeared in all of the top magazines. His recent books include JET PILOT and MIDNIGHT MADONNA.

KILL ME A HUSBAND

TEDD THOMEY

Also published as When the Lusting Began

WILDSIDE PRESS

KILL ME A HUSBAND

chapter 1

She wanted to hurry.

She wanted to race along the sidewalk like a school-girl breathless for adventure, eagerly anticipating what awaited her less than a block away.

But she was not a schoolgirl. She was a woman, a beautiful yellow-haired woman conscious of appearances. Therefore it was necessary for her to stroll, to stop and gaze at a frock in the window of La Ronde's, to walk a few more steps and examine blue china shelved artfully in an adjacent gift shop. And as she turned and beckoned to her seven-year-old daughter, her calm handsome face gave no hint of the ferocious thoughts which were at work behind her blue-green eyes.

"Come on, Eileen," she said impatiently. "Don't hang back so."

The little girl pouted at some glittering rubbish in a dime store window, tossed her blond head and then walked slowly to where her mother was waiting.

"I want a brooch, Mama."

7

"Not today. You're not old enough for a brooch."

"But I just want that little one, that small one with the three little diamonds."

"No. Anyway, they're not diamonds."

"But, Mama, I just—"

"Ask your father."

"Please, Mama!" The pout became more prominent. "You know what he'll say. He never buys me anything and if—"

"Be still, Eileen. Do you want people to look at us?"

"But, Mama, I—"

"*Shut up!*"

The last two words, delivered in a fierce undertone, produced the desired silence. To show her displeasure, the little girl lagged further behind. Her mother strolled on, gazing with disinterest at a trolley which was discharging passengers at the corner, then dropping her eyes to the small gold watch on her slim wrist. She saw that she was still more than thirty minutes early.

She paused at a cigar store window and pretended to be examining a fan-like display of a new petite variety of lady cigarettes. From the corner of her eye, she watched two men seated in the shoe-shine stall next door. One was having his beige Oxfords buffed while the other smoked and read.

She waited. Presently the man who was reading lowered his magazine and glanced at her. She did not look directly at him. She turned to examine a display of white meerschaum pipes, moving just enough to show her figure in full profile. Since it was a warm afternoon in early September, she wore her new marigold-yellow dress, a fashionably cut gown which matched the golden hue of her marcelled hair almost perfectly. It was linen, sleeveless, sufficiently tight across the bodice to achieve an effect which in profile should be quite striking.

She was accorded more reaction than she expected. The man stared at her. Touching his companion with his elbow, he spoke some low words which he concealed behind the rim of his magazine.

Immediately his companion stared at her. The shoe-shine man halted his buffing and turned around.

She let them enjoy themselves for a few seconds. She was certain that when she turned and walked past them they would avert their eyes and feign interest elsewhere.

But they did not. The three continued to gaze at her, open admiration brightening their faces. The man with the magazine sighed loudly and boldly and the shoe-shine man, an Italian with a large curved mustache, grinned at her like a scamp.

More than satisfied, feeling her excitement rising keenly, she walked slowly past. When she was not quite beyond their line of vision, she halted and looked back at her daughter who was dawdling in front of the gift shop window.

"Eileen," she said pleasantly. "I'm waiting, dear."

For a delicious extra moment, she felt their eyes sliding up and down her figure, and then Eileen, who was a well-behaved child, really, joined her and they walked on.

Again she glanced at her watch and saw that she had used up very little additional time. She was still much too early, but now that she was closer to the hotel she found it more difficult to walk slowly. Taking Eileen's hand, she pulled her quickly past a drugstore window, even more quickly past a toy shop window, and then they turned the corner.

Now they were on John Newton Way, the city's most fashionable avenue, and the Newton Hotel rose before them in all its majestic, red-brick glory, its white pillars straight and immaculate in the sunlight. She glanced at the fourth floor, silently counting windows until she noted the most important one, second from the tall center pillar, and she drew in her breath with pleasure. The shade was in the right position, drawn three-fourths of the way down. Her excitement rose even more keenly and was joined by a sensation of wickedness which swirled within her with exquisite sweetness.

9

"Mama, watch out!"

It was Eileen's voice and at the same moment her daughter pulled hard at her arm, drawing her backward, out of the path of a square-roofed Chandler which chugged past, blowing black smoke from its exhaust pipe.

She hadn't been in any danger, really, but she'd been concentrating so thoroughly on the window that she hadn't realized she had stepped off the curb into the street.

"Thank you, dear," she said. "I was daydreaming. Silly of me, wasn't it?"

She laughed and Eileen smiled at her proudly. They continued across the avenue, strolled up the hotel's polished brick steps and entered the cool, silent lobby. Now that she was this close, she was content to walk slowly, even sedately, across the thick carpeting. She touched the broad brim of her yellow picture hat and made certain it rested properly on the yellow waves of her hair. They paused for a moment, impressed by a lavender orchid plant in the doorway of a florist shop which opened onto the lobby, and then they proceeded to one of the leather armchairs grouped around a circular goldfish pool near the elevators.

She waited until Eileen was seated.

"Now I want you to be good," she warned.

"I will, Mama."

"And if you're very, very good, can you guess what I'll buy you?"

"What, Mama?" The child's blue eyes grew round with anticipation.

"A brooch. A better one than that trash in the window."

"Will you, Mama?" Eileen pressed her palms happily to her cheeks. "Honest and truly?"

"Certainly."

From her purse she drew a picture story book and two sticks of clove gum. She handed them to the child with another warning.

"Remember, Eileen. Chew one at a time."

"Yes, Mama. How long will it take?"

"Over an hour, I'm afraid, dear. I need a shampoo as well as a marcel."

"When will you be back?"

"At four." She glanced at her watch. "Possibly four-fifteen."

"All right, Mama. But I hope it doesn't take as long as Monday. I never imagined it would take two hours to do just your nails."

The little girl emphasized her pique with an adult-like shaking of her head and pursing of her lips. "Two hours, *imagine!*"

"That's because I was late, dear. But today I'm early." She raised her finger. "Now you'll be good, won't you?"

"Yes, Mama."

"All right, dear."

She purchased a newspaper for two cents at the central desk, receiving a cozy smile from the handsome young bell captain along with her change. Two other women accompanied her briefly in the elevator, departing for the beauty salon on the mezzanine while she continued on to the fourth floor.

She walked quickly along the corridor, drawing the key to room 440 from her purse, thinking how marvelous it would be if he were already here, waiting for her. The lock turned quietly, she stepped inside and closed the door behind her.

"Bud?" she said softly.

As she waited, enjoying the suspense, she realized she was breathing so rapidly the yellow linen of her bodice was alternately very taut and very loose.

"I'm here," she said. "Bud?"

There was no reply and a faint frown line appeared on her smooth forehead.

She walked to the bathroom door, opened it and switched on the light. He was not there.

Sighing, she returned to the center of the well-furnished room and tossed the newspaper onto the high

11

double bed. She really hadn't expected him to be here early because Wednesday was always his busiest day, but it would have been a nice surprise. She walked to the large picture window which overlooked Newton Way and drew the beige blind the rest of the way down. Then she switched on one of the twin lamps beside the bed, adjusting the shade until a soft pink light was cast on the bedspread.

The full-length mirror near the bed was equipped with its own light. Turning it on, she removed her hat, careful to leave the waves of her hair intact. She smiled at the face in the mirror and it smiled back, revealing clear, well-formed teeth. She recalled the cozy smile the young bell captain had given her, a smile which told her he thought she was close to his own age. She smiled again. No one ever thought she was thirty. Thanks to her Swedish parentage, she was a natural blonde, with that fair, peach-like complexion which never aged.

Her excitement kindled wickedly again as she unhooked her dress and slid it down over her hips. She placed it in careful folds over the back of a chair and slipped from her petticoat and teddy. Stepping from her pumps, she rolled down her garters and silk stockings. She placed the yellow garters upon the dress, arranging them so the gay little black bows were displayed most effectively.

She walked back a few steps until she could see her nude reflection full-length.

Dissatisfied, she shook her head.

She slipped the yellow pumps back onto her feet and re-examined herself in the mirror. Much better. The high heels gave extra length to her beautifully tapered legs. She turned to the right, then to the left, posing finally in a three-quarter view and slowly inhaling.

The sight was impressive. No wonder the three men at the shoe-shine stall had stared for such a long time. Her body was slender except for the breasts. They were not overly large, but they were full and blessed with a lovely upward tilt at the tips. Her legs were long, the thighs

12

full and sensuous, her hips flaring out generously, the flesh cream-colored and satin-smooth.

Expelling her breath slowly, she sighed. It was a shame all this was wasted on Norman, her husband. Norman was such a fool. Busy with his art work, busy with his motorboat, busy with his car, too busy to take advantage of this. She raised herself on tiptoe and watched the muscles of her slim abdomen grow taut. A man would be crazy not to want this. Norman wasn't crazy, not by any means. Nor was he too old. Not for this. Forty-three certainly wasn't too old for this. But he could be so mean and so stubborn. He could be cruel in so many ways that she no longer yielded him the pleasure of her body, not even when he indicated he was interested.

Her blue-green eyes filled with a cold anger. She shouldn't think of Norman. Not now. Not when Bud might arrive at any moment. Thoughts of Norman always filled her with anger and hatred. God, how she hated that man. God, how she hated his methodical, unromantic ways.

She turned from the mirror. From her purse she drew a stick of clove gum, unwrapped it and put it in her mouth. She supposed she shouldn't indulge. Some people said gum-chewing wasn't an attractive habit. But it had a nice taste and it helped when she was feeling nervous. Besides, it would keep her breath sweet for Bud.

She glanced once more at her gold wrist watch. Five minutes after three. What was keeping him? Surely he must know that every moment he delayed was wasted because she would have to be home by five at the latest.

She sat on the side of the bed and picked up the newspaper, glancing only briefly at the dark headlines which told of the dirigible *Shenandoah* being ripped by the wind with a loss of fourteen lives. She turned to the entertainment pages to see what would be playing at the film theaters on Friday when she would not be bothered with Eileen tagging along. She decided she would see Richard Dix and Claire Adams in *Men and Women*. Her girls friends, Mame and Martha, said it was very spicy.

Tossing the newspaper aside, she lay on her back on the bedspread. She raised her feet, touched the toes of her yellow pumps together and admired her nude legs. She certainly had as much to offer as Claire Adams. She wondered what it would be like to make love to Richard Dix and all those other good-looking actors out in California. It would be wonderful to attend parties every night and sleep in a different luxurious bedroom every night, perhaps with a different handsome male every night. If she weren't married to Norman, she could do things like that. Perhaps not on that scale, but different at least from spending an occasional afternoon with Bud and every dreary night with Norman.

God, how she loathed that man. How wonderful it would be to get rid of him. If only she could think of some good way, some easy natural way which would be certain to work.

She frowned at her watch. Now it was ten minutes after. What could be keeping Bud?

She lowered her legs slowly to the chenille spread.

"I'm waiting," she said softly. "Bud, darling, how much longer are you going to keep me waiting?"

chapter 2

Ward Green was definitely not a large man, but he was good-looking in a quiet way and slim enough to wear a double-breasted gray suit which fitted so well it appeared to be custom-tailored, which it was not. He wrote swiftly, filling out the order blank with short decisive strokes of his golden automatic pencil.

"All right, sir," he said, "that takes care of sizes thirty through thirty-four. What about thirty-six and thirty-eight?"

"Well," said the buyer, "I don't know. We'll certainly need at least two dozen thirty-sixes, maybe more."

The buyer placed his elbows on the counter and stared into space, concentrating. "Let me think, Ward. Perhaps four dozen."

Ward revolved the metal pencil nervously in his fingers and gazed at the large clock over the stairway entrance. It was after three, ten minutes after to be exact and he tried desperately to think of some way to conclude the deal quickly without offending the buyer.

15

"How would it be if I came back in the morning?" he said. "That would give you time to think about it."

The buyer, an elderly man with baby-pink cheeks and hair white as sugar, shook his head vigorously.

"Wouldn't think of it, Ward, my boy. How many size thirty-sixes did we buy last September? Four dozen?"

Opening his leather sample case, Ward drew out his record book and turned the pages.

"You have a very good memory, Mr. Trimble. Four dozen is correct. Shall I put down the same figure this time?"

"No, let me think."

Mr. Trimble placed a forefinger against one of his white eyebrows and stared at the floor.

Ward tried not to fidget with his pencil or gold-framed glasses. By exerting extra effort, he kept his features pleasant and relaxed, but inwardly he seethed. He'd promised Alma Chrysler he'd be on time, even told her he might be a little early. Already he was fifteen minutes late and by the time he finished his other errands he would be at least half an hour behind. He dreaded to think how angry she'd be.

"The quality's still the same?" asked Mr. Trimble. "Extra stitching in the larger garments?"

"Yes, sir. And extra stays. There's no better corset made. Shall we say four dozen?"

"Maybe. Let me think."

Mr. Trimble touched his thumbs together thoughtfully Then he touched his little fingers together and pressed even more thoughtfully.

Cursing silently, Ward drew in his breath. He clenched the pencil so tightly his fingers ached.

"All right," said Mr. Trimble. "Four dozen."

Ward scribbled the figure on the order blank and pushed the pad across the counter for Mr. Trimble's signature.

The old man's snowy eyebrows arched with surprise.

"Not yet," he said. "We're not finished yet."

"Sorry," Ward said, more abruptly than he'd intended. "I've got to leave."

"What about the thirty-eights? And the fortys?"

"I'll be back in the morning."

"This is a fine how-de-do—" the old man poised the pencil over the order blank but did not sign it. "What's gotten into you, Ward? You sick or something?"

"I've got another appointment. Are you going to sign it?"

"Maybe I won't." Mr. Trimble's pink lips compressed into a peevish line. "I've never seen you act like this, Ward. Do you want this sale or don't you?"

"Of course. I'll be back in the morning. You can sign it then."

He reached for his golden pencil, but the old man pulled it sharply away.

"Not so fast. Not so fast!"

He scowled at Ward, scowled at the paper, then filled in his signature with slow, deliberate motions.

Ward retrieved the pad and his pencil. He removed the carbon copy clumsily, ripping off one corner. He handed the sheet to Mr. Trimble, closed his leather sample case and turned away from the counter.

"See you in the morning," he said.

He ignored Mr. Trimble's mumbled remark that he might not be available in the morning and plunged past a throng of women fussing around a table covered with cheap sale corsets.

Outside the department store, the sidewalk traffic was thicker than usual and he groaned when he saw the time on a jewelry store clock. Nearly three-thirty. Alma would be pacing the room like a cat. Unless he came up with something good, exactly the right gift, she would make the first few minutes miserable for him.

He hurried along a side street, slowing his footsteps when he came to a small pharmacy with a minimum number of colored apothecary jars and boxed drugs in its single, dingy display window. With a fresh handker-

17

chief he blotted the perspiration from his forehead and glasses, recalling as he did so one of his mother's fond expressions: "A common laborer sweats; a white-collar worker perspires." His mother talked almost continually, everything, but she would be shocked into silence if she quoting the Bible, supplying a favorite expression for knew what he was about to purchase.

Inside the store, which was deserted except for a solitary druggist, he began the proceedings by buying a carton of clove gum and a box of perfumed bath soap.

"And a couple of bottles," he said.

The druggist's quick eyes studied him carefully.

"Bottles of what?"

"All right, all right," Ward said. "Make it the best you've got."

For another moment the druggist continued the scrutiny he undoubtedly awarded all new patrons. Then he shrugged the shoulders of his soiled white jacket.

"It'll have to be rye," he said.

"All right. But hurry up."

"Three dollars."

"I don't care about the price. Just hurry."

"Each," said the druggist.

Ward nodded, placed the money on the glass case and waited while the druggist slipped behind a partition at the rear. After a brief interval he returned with a package wrapped in newspapers which completely failed to disguise its contents. Ward put the package in his sample case and strode from the store.

He wanted to hurry directly to the hotel, but since the department store was on his way, and he was late anyway, he decided another minute's detour would be permissible. He went in a side entrance and kept to the far portion of the main floor to avoid any chance meeting with Mr. Trimble. In the men's room on the second floor, he stepped into a stall, closed the door and unwrapped the two medicine bottles.

He took one drink. It wasn't a long drink, but it was a satisfactory one, the quality of the whiskey being better than he'd anticipated. He left the store by another side entrance, the fashionable one on John Newton Way, and as soon as he stepped out into the sunlight he raised his eyes to the hotel's fourth row of windows.

The blind was no longer in the three-quarters position in which he'd placed it during his visit to the room at noon. It was all the way down. He felt a glow within which was caused only partially by the whiskey.

In the hotel lobby he chose his direction with caution until he located the blond top of Eileen's head. She sat with her small chin resting on her hand, gazing at the goldfish pool. He kept well outside her line of vision as he walked to the elevator, stepping aboard just before the doors closed.

When he was finally in the corridor of the fourth floor, with all the many obstacles of the afternoon safely behind him, his blood began to stir with a rapidity that astonished him. He always felt like this when he knew Alma was near, but each time he was equally astonished at himself. His fingers pushed the key into the lock, but it failed to turn until he withdrew it and inserted it right side up.

The first objects he saw were her clothes, arranged neatly on a chair. He pushed the door shut and strode further into the room.

He glanced across the unoccupied bed to the bathroom door, which was open.

"Alma?" he said.

He walked to the closet door and opened it. There was nothing inside except his unopened suitcase and a few wooden hangers on a wooden pole.

He was not surprised. She did this quite often, and it always added to their pleasure. Today he particularly welcomed the game because it meant she wouldn't be too angry about his tardiness.

"I brought you some presents," he said. "Where are you, Alma?"

There was no reply. He glanced behind the overstuffed Morris chair and then behind the bathroom door.

" *Two* presents," he said cheerfully. "Don't you want them?"

He heard her laughter on the far side of the room, near the window, and turned in time to see a movement behind one of the plum-colored, damask drapes. Crossing over, he chose a portion of drape which displayed a noticeable extra curve and gave it a gentle pinch.

She squealed with delight. Her hands and arms came into view at the edge of the drape and performed an undulating Javanese-like dance with numerous writhing motions of the elbows and wrists. He increased the pressure of his fingers on her hip and she sighed happily in rhythm with the movements of her arms.

"Come out," he said. "Let me see you."

"No." Her tone was mock anger. "I'm mad at you."

"Why?"

"You're terribly late."

"I was delayed with a buyer. Don't you want your presents?"

"No."

"Please come out, Alma. Let me see you."

"No. Not until you say you're sorry."

"I'm sorry, Alma. Terribly sorry."

"That's not enough. Get down on your knees and say it."

Pulling up his trousers to prevent damage to the creases, he dropped to his knees before the drape.

"All right," he said. "I'm very, very sorry."

Her blond head appeared at the side of the drape and her blue-green eyes glared at him hotly.

"Still not enough," she said. "Kiss my foot and say you're sorry."

Her leg, slim and smooth, came from behind the drape and was exposed to the knee. Lifting her foot, he kissed her ankle near the yellow edge of her shoe.

"Not there," she scolded. "On the bottom."

He slipped off her shoe and touched his lips to the smooth skin of her arch.

She sighed. He felt the blood increase its beat at his temples.

"Are you my slave?" she demanded.

"Yes." He kept his head bowed.

"You will do anything I tell you to do?"

"Yes."

"All right. You're forgiven."

Looking up, he saw that she had drawn the drape tightly across her body, molding the plum-colored material to her figure like an expensive gown. His excitement rose sharply. He stood up and tugged at the drape, revealing part of her shoulder.

"No," she said, drawing the cloth back over her skin, "not till I see the presents."

He handed her the box of perfumed soap.

"Smells heavenly." She smiled. "Come here."

She kissed him on the cheek.

"And a little something else," he said, handing her the gum.

"A whole box! You shouldn't have, darling!"

"Sugar for my sugar," he said.

"Oh, Bud, you darling! You say the prettiest things!"

She kissed him on the cheek again, this time closer to his mouth. He put his arms around her and kissed her on the lips. Her mouth was very warm. Something struck the rug near his feet and as her arms came around him he realized she had dropped the boxes of soap and gum. Her hands caressed his neck and cheek.

"Oh, Bud, darling," she said. "You're so good for me. So very good."

He tugged at the drape, but it was caught between them. He pulled harder. As it came free he thrust it away from them.

She danced away from his grasp, turned and let him gaze at her nudeness, standing with her left foot on tiptoe to make up for the absence of its yellow slipper. As always, the first look at her magnificent body took his breath away. Her breasts had an astonishing tilted beauty which she emphasized by drawing her shoulders back. Her abdomen was slender, the skin silky, the slightly irregular appendectomy scar providing a fascinating distraction. Her eyes were full of fire and her cheeks, usually a light apricot color, were flushed with color and excitement.

He reached for her, gently fondled her left breast, and she gave a small cry of pleasure.

"You damned devil," she said. "You kept me waiting so long!"

With sudden force, she threw herself against him. Her legs twined around his and he tripped. He dropped to one knee, balanced momentarily, but she thrust herself harder against him and he tumbled backward onto the rug. It was not a hard fall and she was upon him at once, kissing his forehead, his cheeks, his chin and mouth, her warm nakedness covering his body and setting up a tumult of sensation that was all-engulfing.

Her fingers moved swiftly, tearing open his collar, unbuttoning his shirt, kindling his excitement to unendurable heights.

"You darling devil!" she said, as their eager hands took their will of each other's yielding flesh. "I'll teach you to keep me waiting so long!"

And then, their arms and legs entwined, their bodies fused into one, their moist mouths hotly joined, they lost themselves in a dizzying whirl of sensation.

Later they sat side by side on the bed, shoulders resting against the headboard, the top sheet covering them lightly.

"More?" he said, tilting the bottle toward her glass.

"I better not." She set her glass on the nightstand. "Norman might get suspicious."

"I thought you said he's never suspicious."

"He never seems to be. But you can't tell about him. He seems so dumb, never asking about where I've been, never caring. And then he'll do something so mean it makes me wonder."

"Has he done something else?"

"Yes."

"What?"

"He hit me with his fist. Here."

Leaning forward, she indicated an area between her shoulderblades.

"Is there a bruise?"

"I don't see one. Turn a little more and I'll fix it for you."

She turned, keeping the sheet draped across her front, but revealing all of her back which narrowed beautifully to her waist. He kissed the spot she had indicated and felt her shiver as he drew his lips away.

"Better?" he said.

"Much better, darling."

She smiled, but only briefly. She clenched her teeth and the smooth line of her jaw became more pronounced.

"God, how I hate him!"

He nodded sympathetically, his pale cheeks taking on a hint of color.

"If only I wasn't married to him. If only something would—" She hesitated, then turned and faced him, her eyes narrowed and intent. "Did I tell you what happened last Friday night?"

"No. What?"

"Him and his damned boat and his damned car, that's all he ever thinks about, or talks about. He was out in the garage, lying underneath the new Essex he's so proud of, changing the grease or something. All of a sudden the jack slipped and the whole car came down."

"Did he get hurt?"

"No, worse luck! The wheel missed his head by an inch."

"You shouldn't say that." Bud's voice registered shock.

"Say what?"

"Say worse luck, like that."

"Oh, I shouldn't?" Her eyes became fiery with anger. "After the things he's done to me? I'll say more than that! I'll say I wish he was out of my life, gone, buried, anything!"

He stared at her, surprised at her intensity.

"That's an awful thing to say, Alma."

"I don't care. I hate him. I wish he was buried!"

His surprise gave way to consternation. "Alma, you shouldn't! Don't you know what that means in the eyes of God?"

"I don't care! And you should hate him, too!"

"Me? I've never even met him."

"But you should, Bud. You should hate him." Sliding closer to him on the bed, Alma kissed the side of his neck. "Couldn't you hate him a little, for my sake?"

He put his arms around her and caressed her body through the thin sheet.

"I suppose so, Alma."

"You devil—" Her teeth fastened on the flesh of his neck and remained there a moment, inflicting a pleasant pain. 'Are you trying to start the fire all over again, darling?"

"Yes. I can't help it."

"You're really sweet. I could just go on loving you and loving you but—" She glanced at her wrist watch. "My God, it's after five! I've got to fly!"

She hurried from the bed and began to put on her clothes.

"I hate to run, darling, but I must. Poor little Eileen must be wondering what's happened!"

Watching her slide with graceful ease into her white petticoat, Bud wondered how he had ever managed to win the love of such a beautiful and exciting woman. It was a question he had pondered many times during the three months he had known her. Everything she did was exciting. Even the way she fastened the hooks on her dress was exciting.

He stepped from the bed and pressed his face against the yellow waves of her hair.

"Don't go, Alma."

"Stop it." She gave him a quick, affectionate squeeze. "Don't touch me again or you know what'll happen. But I must go, Bud, really."

"Friday?" he asked, his eyes and voice eager.

"Of course."

"Same time?"

"Yes, darling."

She picked up her yellow hat and purse. "And don't keep me waiting, understand?"

"I won't, dear."

She hurried to the door, opened it, slammed it and was gone.

Sitting down on the bed, he gazed at the door and sighed. She was amazing. Even the way she'd slammed the door was exciting.

chapter 3

Wednesday night Norman did not go near the garage, preferring to spend the hours after dinner romping in the yard with Eileen and the dog.

But when he arrived home from the office on Thursday night he announced that the car's timing was off and that he was going to fix it.

"Tonight?" complained Alma's mother, Mrs. Jansson. "Do you have to fix it tonight?"

"Yes."

"But you're supposed to take me and Eileen to the church play."

"Sorry."

Alma made no comment. She glanced coldly at her husband and continued setting the table.

During the meal there was little conversation and Norman left the table just as Mrs. Jansson arrived from the kitchen bearing a pan of hot cinnamon rolls which she had baked especially for him.

"Sit back down, Norman," she said. "This is your favorite dessert and if you think you—"

"Sorry. Work to be done."

Alma clenched her teeth and kept silent. He could be hateful in so many small, deliberate ways. She watched him walk to the hall and reach for his khaki work smock. He was a big man, slightly over six feet, making him five inches taller than Bud. In a way he was better-looking than Bud because his features were strong and more masculine. As he pushed his arms into the sleeves of the smock, his movements were slow and methodical, totally unlike Bud's who was so quick and deft with his hands. And yet, strangely, Norman's hands were the more skilled money-wise, his talent with pencil and ruler earning him an excellent salary at the publishing house where he was art editor.

After Norman went outside, the two women and Eileen remained at the table for a few minutes eating the rolls and sipping tea. Alma helped her mother clear the dishes and then she went into the sitting room while Mrs. Jansson and Eileen finished up in the kitchen.

She picked up a magazine and tried to continue with the love story she'd been reading before dinner, but she was unable to concentrate. She thought about Bud and her pulse quickened as she remembered how much pleasure they'd had the day before. And tomorrow afternoon might be even more enjoyable.

She frowned as the engine of the Essex started up. It raced madly for a moment, the sound coming clearly into the sitting room even though the garage was out back and separated from the house. Then it backfired loudly and stopped.

The phone rang.

Eileen came dashing from the kitchen to answer it, but Alma was there a step before her.

"Hello?" She hoped it was Bud, although she had told him more than once never to phone in the evening.

"Alma?"

It was Mame, one of her girl friends.

"Yes," Alma said. "How's everything?"

"Fine. Say, Alma, there's a keen one at the Liberty

27

tonight with Edmund Lowe and Carole Lombard. How's if I phone up Martha and we make it a threesome?"

"Tonight?" Alma paused. " 'Fraid not, Mame. I've got a lot to catch up on tonight."

"Heavy date?"

"No, not tonight."

"How are you and Ward Green getting along? I hear you've been pretty chummy lately."

"All right, I guess."

"Only all right?" Mame giggled. "That ain't the way I've been hearing it. His pal Ralphie has been telling me that Ward and—"

"Please, Mame. Some other time."

"Oh, all right, spoil my fun. How about a movie next Tuesday instead?"

"Sounds fine. Give me a ring."

"O.K. 'Bye."

" 'Bye."

When Alma returned to her chair, the car's engine was sputtering and backfiring, filling the house with noise. She picked up her magazine but did not open it. Instead she gazed past the top of the floor lamp to the framed photograph centered on the sitting room's most prominent wall. It was the portrait of a girl of twenty, with large, sensitive eyes and a sad mouth. *Poor Winifred*, she thought. *You'll never know how lucky you were to escape all this.*

In a few minutes, Mrs. Jansson and Eileen came in, donning sweaters because the September evening had turned chilly. Beneath the sweater Mrs. Jansson wore her cotton housedress and sturdy white cotton stockings.

"We'll have to hurry," she said. "It's a long walk to the church."

She sighed. It was the sigh of a woman of fifty who wore her widowhood well, but who occasionally lapsed into small displays of self-pity. She was still quite good-looking, although her short blond hair was fading and there was more than a hint of good Swedish heaviness around her hips. Her face was similar to Alma's—nose small, brow-line excellent, complexion clear. It was only in recent years that a few wrinkles had appeared near her eyes and beneath her strong chin.

" 'Bye, Mommy," Eileen said.

Alma waved as they went out, then covered her ears with her palms as the sound of more explosive back-firing came in through the open door.

She read for perhaps a quarter of an hour. Then she walked to the dining room window and drew aside the lacy curtain. The light which streamed from the garage's open doors showed Norman leaning on the Essex's high fender, head bent over the engine. From the exhaust came coiling clouds of black smoke.

Opening the glass-doored buffet, she took down two shot glasses of different sizes and a pint flask of whiskey. She filled the larger glass to the brim and put considerably less in the smaller one. She put the glasses on a tray, walked to the kitchen and filled a tumbler with tap water. Placing it beside the whiskey glasses, she went outside.

He scowled as she approached. Then he noticed what was on the tray and his expression changed to mild surprise.

"What's that for?" he said.

"It's chilly. I thought you might be cold."

His greasy fingers picked up the larger glass and he downed its contents in one swallow, chasing it with a gulp of water.

He did not thank her. Turning back to the engine, he made an adjustment which caused it to sputter and gasp like a large animal unable to breathe enough air. She watched him for a few minutes, sipping from her glass, then she returned to her chair in the sitting room.

But now she was unable to remain still. She walked idly around the room, straightening an embroidered doily on the sofa, rearranging the Swedish bric-a-brac on the corner shelf. As her fingers moved, the stone in her engagement ring twinkled and she thought back to the night Norman had presented it to her. Eleven years ago.

29

Eleven wasted years. Even then she hadn't loved him. But it had been a large diamond, the largest she'd ever seen, much too large to be ignored by a nineteen-year-old girl who didn't know the full meaning of the word love. A nineteen-year-old girl who soon, however, learned the full meaning of the word hate.

She paused beneath the photograph of Winifred. Now she felt no pity for Winifred, only hate. For eleven years she had lived with this portrait of Norman's dead fiancée. He had hung it in a prominent place in each of their homes, starting with their honeymoon flat on West Fourth Street. He had made it clear more than once that she was merely a substitute for Winifred. Always when their arguments grew most violent he mentioned Winifred and what a much better wife she would have made.

Winifred, Winifred, Winifred . . . He'd even put Winifred's name on his motorboat and there had been weeks of dispute, weeks of tears, until he consented, bitterly, to paint out the word *Winifred* and replace it with *Alma*, in smaller letters.

Winifred, Winifred . . . She felt her fingernails pressing sharply into the flesh of her clenched fists.

She hated Winifred, hated her with every fiber of her being. Winifred had been dead for many years, yet in this house she had been kept tormentingly alive. And in Norman's mind she was still the same sweet fiancée of scarcely twenty, unchanged, sensitive, still so very virginal. And how Norman loved to hint about Winifred's virginity. How proud he was of Winifred's virginity. The fool. As if that was anything to be proud of.

She cursed him. Her hatred for Winifred was great, but it was nothing compared to her deep and violent hatred for him. Because the portrait of Winifred and the constant mentions of Winifred's superiority were only two of the numerous cruelties he practiced.

Most of them were smaller cruelties, but just as deliberate. But the worst of all was his coldness, the pride he took in not caring what she did with herself day after day, not caring about what happened to her.

She cursed him. Then she went to the tray and with trembling fingers refilled his glass with whiskey.

When she returned to the garage, he was lying beneath the quietly idling car. With her foot she nudged his nearest leg where it protruded from under the running board. He crawled partway clear of the car and frowned up at her from the floor.

"Now what?"

She knelt beside him. "It's getting colder. I thought you might like another."

For a moment there was puzzlement in his gray eyes and she could guess what he was thinking. Tonight was the first time she had ever brought the tray to the garage and anything which wasn't routine bothered him. But since he was used to being waited on, demanding constant service from her mother as well as herself, she was certain his puzzlement would be brief.

She was right. He reached for the glass, downed the whiskey and followed it with a swallow of water.

"Nearly got her fixed," he said. "Notice how quiet she's running?"

She nodded.

He crawled back under the car and Alma walked outside to the yard. But she did not go into the house. For a few minutes she stood in the darkness near the kitchen porch. Whiskey always made him drowsy. The two glasses had contained a larger amount than usual and his drowsiness should commence a little sooner.

She shivered as a chill breeze pierced the thin cloth of her housedress and dashed a handful of dry leaves against the fence.

She walked back to the garage. Quietly she closed the left-hand door, noting that he was still working beneath the car. The hinges of the right-hand door squeaked as she pushed it shut, but she was certain the sound was muffled by the idling engine.

31

Hurrying across the yard, she did not look back at the garage. When she returned to her chair in the sitting room, her heart was beating so rapidly it felt like a bird trying to escape from within the walls of her chest. Rarely had she known such excitement. It was exquisite, equal even to that she had enjoyed with Bud yesterday afternoon.

She picked up her magazine, but almost immediately laid it aside. Her fingers felt cold and she rubbed them together. She glanced at her watch and realized the doors had been closed less than two minutes. It seemed so much longer.

She walked once around the room. She stopped at the buffet and filled the smaller shot glass with whiskey. She drank half, paused a moment, and finished it. The liquor was pleasantly warm, but it was not what she wanted, after all. Opening the top buffet drawer, she drew out a package of gum and put one of the clove sticks in her mouth.

She chewed hard. She chewed in rhythm with the swift beat of her heart. Almost at once she felt better, felt in control of her nerves once more.

Striding to the portrait of Winifred, she stared coldly at the young, wistful face, chewing the gum with short, rapid movements of her jaw.

The excitement was becoming almost too much. She found that she could not bear to stand in one place. It was much easier to walk around the room, to circle the room again and again and think only about how she loathed everything about Norman.

Exactly seven minutes had passed when she heard the abrupt sound in the yard.

She was close enough to the dining room window to see light streaming once again from the garage because the doors were open and swinging on their hinges.

Norman was leaning against the car trunk, shaking his head violently from side to side.

He walked away from the garage, coming toward the house with unsteady, weaving footsteps.

When he came in through the side door, she was seated in her chair, eyes upon her magazine.

She heard him stumble against the sewing machine, but she did not look up. Her heart was beating so loudly she was certain he would hear it.

Gasping and coughing, he dropped heavily onto the sofa. He pounded his chest with his fist.

"What's the matter with you?" she said.

He did not reply until his coughing subsided.

"Gas," he said. "Monoxide."

Clearing his throat, he spat into his handkerchief. Then he looked at her, but there was no accusation or suspicion in his eyes.

"God damn wind," he said. "Blew the doors shut on me!"

She walked over to the buffet, filled a glass with whiskey and took it to him.

"You should be more careful," she said.

chapter 4

Not until two months later, in November, were Alma and Ward able to arrange an entire night together. For Ward it had been a day of continual rushing, winding up corset sales early in several specialty shops, almost missing his train, finally meeting Alma for a late supper in downtown Manhattan.

It was ten o'clock before they'd reached the suite she had rented in the La Paloma Hotel.

Now it was nearly midnight and she was still in her strange mood.

"I just don't want to make love," she said.

"But why, Alma? What's the matter?" His face was tinged with worry.

"I just don't feel like it."

"But why?"

She did not answer. Instead she shrugged, picked up her film magazine and sat on the chesterfield, her legs folded comfortably beneath her. She stroked the arm rest, which was brown brocade with a heavy gold thread.

"Isn't this nice material?" she said. "You still haven't told me how you like the suite."

"But I did, Alma. It was the first thing I mentioned when we came in."

"Oh, did you?" She turned the magazine's pages idly, not looking at them, but not looking at him, either.

Ward was completely baffled by her attitude. For weeks they had planned this date, their first night together. They had exchanged numerous notes and phone calls, deciding that the Friday after Thanksgiving would be the easiest to arrange because Norman would be away on a fishing trip. Norman was always the complication; Ward's wife was never a problem because she was used to his being away on sales trips. Finally everything had been worked out. All during the hectic, long day he had looked forward eagerly to tonight, thinking about the pleasures they would share, thinking about her amazing body.

He sat down on the chesterfield beside her. He reached toward her knee which was partially exposed below the hem of her black party dress. Almost immediately she twisted away from him, tucking both knees out of reach.

His frustration turned to anger and as it rose bitterly within him he realized it was the first time he'd ever felt this way toward her. And it was all so foolish. There was absolutely no reason for it.

He crashed his palms together angrily and strode away from the chesterfield. Standing before the glass-topped bureau, he poured himself a large drink of whiskey, added a little water, and downed a good portion of it in the first swallow. Over the rim of the tumbler, he studied himself in the bureau mirror. There was nothing wrong with his appearance. His white shirt was fresh, his red and black tie was knotted correctly and he had shaved on the train for the second time today in order to be presentable.

Finishing the drink, he set the tumbler down on the bureau top with an emphatic click. It was his third drink, or possibly his fourth, and he waited a moment, letting it settle within him, adding fuel to his anger, building up his confidence.

Abruptly he turned away from the bureau.

"God damn it!" he said. "I want to know what's the matter!"

He was surprised at his tone. It was strong, almost authoritative, totally unlike the usual sound of his voice.

Alma looked up from her magazine.

"Why, Bud," she said. "Shame on you."

"What for?" he demanded.

"I thought you never took the Lord's name in vain." Her words were softly mocking. "I didn't think you ever swore."

"God damn it, I will if I want to!" Pushing his fists deep into his trousers pockets, he strode back to the chesterfield and glared down at her. He knew the whisky was making him act this way and he welcomed the change in himself, even if it might only be temporary. "Now what the hell's the matter? Is it me? Is it something I've done?"

"Partly."

She smiled a mysterious feminine smile that told him nothing.

"All right, damn it," he said. "What have I done?"

Her smile became warmer. "I like you when you act this way, Bud. So masculine. Now you sit down and I'll tell you what's the matter."

He started to sit beside her on the chesterfield, but she restrained him.

"No, Bud. On the floor. Here." She pointed to the rug directly before her. "You see, dear, I want to run my fingers through your hair."

As soon as he sat on the floor, he knew it was a mistake, another sign of weakness, because somehow her higher position on the chesterfield automatically robbed him of authority. But as he leaned back, closing his eyes, feeling her fingers stroking his hair, he decided that if it was a mistake it was certainly a very enjoyable one.

36

"I love your hair, Bud. It's so thick, so wavy, and exactly the color of autumn leaves. And you keep it so neat, not all shaggy like Norman."

Her fingers stroked his forehead and then lightly touched other parts of his face.

"You have a very good forehead, Bud. It's high and that's a mark of intelligence." She toyed with the gold frame of his glasses. "And these are a mark of intelligence, too. But best of all I think I love your chin. Did I ever tell you that you're the only man I've ever known that had a cleft chin?"

"I don't think so."

"Well, it's true. I think your chin is just perfect."

Her fingers explored the cleft lightly, enticingly, and as he kissed her palm, he felt an urge to draw her down beside him, to embrace and fondle her. But when he tugged gently at her arm, she resisted and drew her arm away.

He tried to rise, but her hands caught his shoulders.

"No," she said. "Stay there while I finish. I love meeting you like this, Bud, darling. I love spending the night with you. It's very exciting. And I don't mind having to pay for the suite because Norman's got plenty of money. And if you want me to lend you another twenty-five, I'll be glad to, as you well know."

"Thank you, dear." He placed his palm over hers where it rested on his shoulder. "Business sure has been rotten."

"I know. But, Bud, darling, you must realize that I'm the one that's taking the greater risk. You realize, don't you, that the man always has it the easiest? And it's the woman who suffers if anything should go wrong?"

"Yes, I suppose so."

"I'm glad you do, Bud. And that's why I wanted to have this little talk. I feel that you owe me something— and I don't mean money—for what I've given you. And what I want to give you."

"Of course, Alma." Turning, he noted that her large,

blue-green eyes were somber, more serious than he had ever seen them. "What is it that you want, Alma? Is something the matter, is something worrying you?"

"Yes."

"What? Is it Norman?"

"Partly."

"Is there something you want me to do?"

"Yes."

"What?"

"I want you to promise something."

"Of course, Alma, darling. All you have to do is name it."

"All right, dear. I want you to promise to help me."

"To do what?"

"I want you to promise to help me no matter what happens. I want you to promise to stand by me and help me if I should need you."

"Of course, dear. But what are you afraid of? What do you think might happen?"

"Do you promise?"

"Yes, of course."

"Will you promise on the Bible?"

"Of course."

"Then get that one over there." She pointed to the mahogany writing desk where a Gideon Bible was displayed.

"All right."

He brought the book to her and they placed both their palms upon it.

"Do you swear to help me?" Her eyes were deeply concerned. "Do you swear to help me if ever I need you?"

"Yes, Alma. I swear it."

"Thank you, darling. I feel so relieved."

She rose from the chesterfield and kissed him on the lips. "In fact, I feel wonderful. Let's have some fun! Let's have a party!"

She tossed the Bible into the air and it landed upside

down on the chesterfield, cover open, its own weight wrinkling the thin pages.

Pulling up her skirt, she kicked off her high-heeled pumps, sending them skidding across the rug.

"Fix me another drink, Bud!" She snatched her empty glass from the end table and expertly flipped it to him. "Fix me a big sexy drink!"

While he poured the whisky into their glasses, she rubbed her hip against him, with slow, cat-like motions. They laughed as he spilled some of the liquor. After touching their glasses together, they drank, kissed, drank and kissed some more.

Alma finished her drink first. She unwrapped a stick of chewing gum, put it in her mouth and gave him another kiss.

"Whisky and clove," she said. "Sexy?"

"Very much so!" He felt the blood beating heavily against his throat and now he was glad that she had delayed like this and put him off because it was more exciting this way, a dozen times more exciting. He reached for her, but before he could touch her wonderful breasts, she twisted quickly away from him and went toward the chesterfield.

She bounced on the cushions, then climbed to the arm rest, standing with her arms stretched overhead, moving her hips slowly from side to side.

He ran toward her, but she squealed happily and pushed him away.

"Not yet, Bud!"

Unfastening the hooks on her dress, she started to pull it over her head, but as soon as it covered her eyes she lost her balance and teetered to and fro on the arm rest.

He stared at her, totally entranced because there had been no hint at any time during the evening that she wore nothing under the black party dress.

She slipped off the arm rest and fell across the chesterfield, half in the dress, half out.

"Bud," she giggled, "help me!"

He leaned over her, hesitating. Then he drew the Bible from under her knee, closed it and placed it on the end table.

"Hurry, Bud. I'm smothering!"

Tugging at the dress, he pulled it over her head and dropped it to the rug. He fell to the cushions beside her, embracing her, kissing her eyes and her warm, flushed cheeks.

"Not yet!" She laughed and pushed him away. "Not yet!"

Once more she leaped to the arm rest, standing with arms outstretched, completely nude except for her silk stockings which were rolled just below the knee, held in place with circular yellow garters. She chewed her gum with rapid motions, lips parted, teeth shining in the light from the cut-glass chandelier.

"Am I pretty?" she demanded.

"Yes!"

"Are you excited?"

"Yes, damn it!" He rose to his knees on the chester-field and reached toward her. "You're driving me crazy!"

"Do I look like a bride?"

"Yes, damn it!"

"Then catch me, Daddy, because here I come!"

She leaped into his arms and they sprawled across the cushions, side by side. She fastened her teeth into the cords of his neck, biting so hard he felt the pain all the way to his shoulder.

"How did you like that, Daddy?"

"I loved it, Mommy. Do it again!"

She bit him once more, equally hard, and he wrapped his arms around her and held her tight. They kissed as if driven by demands and compulsions which would never be calmed. He stroked his palms hard against the silkiness of Alma's naked flesh, finding the contours and smooth hollows, and he felt her body grow tense with desire and felt himself being drawn to exceptional heights of sensation. She pulled him savagely against her. And as their bodies united in the age-old rhythm of love, there was only one reality, their demand for each other, their hurtling, aching need for fulfillment.

"Oh, my God," he cried. "I love you, Mommy!"

He slept as if drugged—a deep sleep which was totally dark except for a pinpoint of light twinkling in the distance. As the light came closer, growing larger, he knew he was beginning to dream and he tried to turn his head, tried to avoid looking at the light. But he could not. The light became brighter and brighter and as it drew closer he felt a heavy sensation of guilt. Again he tried to turn away, but the light mesmerized him, making him hold his neck muscles rigid. And now it was so close that he could identify it and his guilt was a tremendous weight within him. Because the light was a halo. And directly beneath it was a woman in white robes—long white robes that swept the ground as she walked toward him. And in her pale white hands she carried reverently a Bible with wrinkled pages. He tried to cry out. He tried to say "No! No!" But he could not speak.

As the woman came closer he saw that she was his mother and the halo shone brightly upon her white hair and upon the tragic expression of her face. She took one more step toward him and abruptly, like a picture projected by a magic lantern, her face was replaced by another. The new face was Alma's, wicked and wanton, chewing gum, her tongue flicking pinkly against her teeth. Just as abruptly the face changed again. And now it was Peony's face, pink and very youthful—Peony of the plump lips and baby chin. And Peony was laughing at him, pointing her finger at him and laughing uproariously, peals of laughter that crashed against his eardrums and reverberated within the coves and corridors of his brain.

He awoke so quickly his body was stiff for a moment, his legs aching from the strain. Unable to determine at

41

once where he was, he gazed about the dim room, blinking at the strange shapes. He turned his head and saw Alma lying beside him on the bed and then he remembered. He felt very tired. Recalling the dream, he forced his eyes to remain open because he didn't want to dream like that again. The guilt lay within him as heavy as his exhaustion. He was not dismayed by the appearance in his dream of his mother with the Bible. It was rather remarkable that she had remained silent instead of admonishing him and quoting the Seventh Commandment, "Thou Shalt Not Commit Adultery," and perhaps several others. Nor had the appearance of Alma surprised him.

But Peony had been a definite shock. He had not though about Peony for a long time. Peony with her plump fifteen-year-old figure. Peony with her plump lower lip and her laughter.

He stared at the dim ceiling. It wasn't right for Peony to laugh in the dream and ridicule him. He didn't want to remember how it had been, but his mind went back anyway, recalling how he had pursued Peony into the tall grass on the slopes behind the school. He had been seventeen at the time and he had heard the other fellows talking more than once about how easy Peony was. He had been amazed when she whispered to him after school and flicked her white skirts at him. He was amazed that she had chosen him, the smallest boy in the junior class and easily the most quiet.

He had walked with her silently up the slopes, his heart drumming because she stayed so close beside him, her leg touching his more than once as they moved into the taller grass. Once when he helped her through the strands of a wire fence she deliberately pressed her left breast, very young and very firm, against his arm and he had grown so excited he had lost his footing and nearly fallen.

He closed his eyes tightly, trying to erase the image, but it would not erase. He could still see Peony's face, pink and soft-chinned, the eyes baby blue but not at all

42

innocent. She selected a place where the grass was waist high and then she winked at him—winked at him with a wickedness which was far too knowing for her fifteen years, and she held out her arms to him.

He had stared at her, unable to move.

"Are you just going to stand there?" she demanded.

"What do you mean?" He knew it was the wrong thing to say, but he could not help himself.

"Aren't you going to kiss me? Don't you want to?"

"Sure," he said. "Sure, Peony—"

He had fumbled against her, somehow finding her lips in his excitement and was astonished at how moist and strange her mouth felt. It was the first time he had ever kissed a girl. Almost at once she had begun moving her hip against him, caressing him with it, and then she had pulled him down into the tall soft grass.

"Isn't this nice here?" she whispered. "Doesn't it make you want to do things?"

"Sure," he said. "Sure, but—"

"You're just shy," she said. "Here, I'll show you."

But as her hand took his and placed it upon her breast, he felt terror instead of desire and drew away.

"What's the matter with you?"

"Nothing."

"Then come here."

She lay back in the grass, her eyes glittering at him while her hands drew her skirt slowly up, revealing her white plump thighs.

He had wanted to touch her. He had wanted desperately to touch her soft stomach and legs but instead he had panicked. He had gotten quickly to his feet and retreated from her.

"Come back here!" she ordered.

"No!"

"Come here!"

"No, I'm sorry, Peony, but I—"

She had insisted. She had scolded. And then she began the insults. And the laughter.

43

"Sissy!" she said. "Fraidy cat!"

He fled from her, running down the slopes, hearing her sarcastic laughter all the way, hearing more insults.

"Sissy! Sissy!" she'd called. "Run to your mother, sissy!"

Her laughter had followed him all the way to the road and it rang in his ears even after he was home. The next day he had not gone to school because he knew Peony would tell and the boys would whisper about him and laugh behind his back. Nor did he return to school on subsequent days. Instead he took a job at the packing house, sweeping floors and carrying cartons. He never returned to school.

Turning over, he tried to sleep, but the dream and his thoughts of Peony remained sharply in his mind. Silently he cursed the dream. It was wrong for the dream to mock him with Peony's laughter. Not tonight, not here in this room where he had certainly proved himself as a man.

He felt Alma stir beside him and then she whispered softly in his ear.

"Are you awake?"

He did not answer.

"Bud?"

Her finger touched first one rib, then another, moving provocatively.

"Bud," she said. "Wake up!"

He pretended to stretch and awaken, then turned and looked at her. Her eyes seemed to shine in the darkness.

She giggled. She poked him with her finger.

"Let's have a party," she said.

He expelled his breath with a rush.

"Again?" he said.

"Why not? Aren't you my ever-loving Buddy-boy?"

"Yes, but—"

"No buts." Her warm mouth nuzzled his ear and her hand began to caress his leg. "Am I your ever-loving Mommy-girl?"

"Yes, dear. Of course."

44

He could not resist.

Nor did he want to resist, not when he thought of Peony and her sarcastic laughter.

chapter 5

She bustled about the living room, turning down a fold on the flowered cover on the sofa, straightening the edges of the pile of film magazines and making sure there was no dust on the window sill.

"Goodness, Alma." Her mother smiled at her fondly. "I can't get over how good you've been looking the last few months. Do you really think that new medicine, that awful-tasting stuff, is making such a change in you?"

"Of course, Mother. It's full of iron and pep, that's what the doctor says."

Mrs. Jansson wrinkled her nose. "I suppose I ought to try taking some again. But I just can't abide that rotten-egg taste."

"Don't worry about it," Alma said. "I'll be getting a new bottle when I see the doctor on Monday. Maybe it won't taste as bad."

She smoothed her skirt and then patted Mrs. Jansson's cheek. "Be sure and take your apron off. Mr. Green said he'll be here at eleven-thirty."

"I wish you hadn't told him to come." Mrs. Jansson

sighed and shook her head. "My goodness, I don't even wear the corsets I've got, so why bother with a new one?"

"Now, Mother, you know you should do something about your figure. And when I see the doctor Monday I'll ask him if you should try some more of the medicine. I think it's been helping Norman."

"Well, maybe you do know best. But the taste—"

Mrs. Jansson stopped talking as the phone rang.

"Oh, dear," said Alma. "I hope it's not Mr. Green saying he can't come."

She walked into the hallway and took the receiver off the hook.

"Hello?" She kept her voice low so her mother wouldn't overhear.

"Howdy, honey! Got a sec to talk?"

It was the bright, lively voice of Scotty McNally. She had told him before, and Ralph too, never to call her at home. They were both building contractors, working for the same big company, and they were lots of fun at times, wonderful fun. But they just didn't realize that she didn't have as much time for them these days because of Ward.

"No, I can't talk," she said. "I'll call you this afternoon."

"Only need a sec, baby. How about a little get-together Monday P.M.?"

"No, Scotty. I'm always dated up on Mondays, Wednesdays and Fridays. I've told you that before."

"So you have, hon. So you have. How about Tuesday?"

Trying to decide, she hesitated. She had known Scotty much longer than Ward and it wasn't easy to tell him no because he could be very persistent and difficult, employing a variety of sales talks.

"Scotty," she said, "I'll call you back. Really, this is the wrong time to call. I'm going to hang up now. 'Bye."

Replacing the phone, she returned to the front room.

"Who was it?" her mother asked.

"Mame. Her and her movies. I told her I couldn't go."

"Did she say which one she'd been to last?"

"No."

"I wish she had. I was thinking I might go to one this afternoon after I shop."

"Why don't you, Mother. Take a little out of the grocery money and have a soda while you're at it."

"Thank you, Alma." Mrs. Jansson smiled, delighted with her daughter's generosity. "You're really too good to me—I just don't know where I'd be without you—"

Through the living room window Alma saw a movement on the front steps.

"He's here, Mother. Now you be nice to him, won't you?"

"Of course, dear. But I still don't know why you should buy me another corset. My gracious, Alma, they're so uncomfortable, so tight around the—"

"Mother, please!"

Alma put her finger to her lips and Mrs. Jansson nodded and kept silent.

The bell rang and Alma opened the front door.

"Why how do you do, Mr. Green. It's so nice of you to come."

She winked at him.

He winked back.

"Good morning, Mrs. Chrysler. I trust that I haven't kept your mother waiting?"

"Not at all. Please come in."

It went off very well. She saw at once that her mother was impressed by this neat-suited stranger with the clean fingernails and good manners. Ward was actually only a few inches taller than Mrs. Jansson, but he always looked considerably taller than he was because his thick reddish-brown hair was combed in an erect, wavy pompadour. At no time did he touch Mrs. Jansson and this propriety won her over completely. He allowed her to measure herself with his tape in the privacy of the hallway. He referred to the sample garments from his leather case as corselets and kept his eyes carefully

48

averted while Mrs. Jansson managed an intimate inspection of the seams and stays.

After the purchase was made, and a date set for delivery of the garment, Mrs. Jansson looked at the mantel clock and then at her daughter.

"Alma," she said, "it's almost noon. Don't you think we should invite Mr. Green to lunch?"

"What a nice idea," Alma said. "I should have thought of it myself."

"I'll fix it," Mrs. Jansson said. "You two just sit here and talk."

For an hour, until after one o'clock, Alma and Ward dawdled over their chicken pies, salad and muffins. At that point Mrs. Jansson, as Alma knew she would, announced that she was late for her shopping trip, apologizing to Mr. Green for not being able to stay until lunch was over.

"You go right ahead," Ward said sociably. "I'll be leaving in a few minutes myself, but not until I have one more cup of this delicious Swedish coffee."

That compliment, following several others, completed Mrs. Jansson's capitulation and she departed with a smile, inviting Mr. Green to stay as long as he liked and enjoy several more cupfuls. Alma watched from the window and as soon as Mrs. Jansson's solid figure was out of sight, she skipped across the room and seated herself on Ward's lap.

"Right on schedule," she giggled. "Didn't I tell you?"

He kissed her throat and then touched her nose with the tip of his tongue. "You're a genius, Mommy. How long will she be gone?"

"Hours, darling. All afternoon, at least."

She mussed his hair, loosened his collar and bit him playfully on the neck. Then she wriggled off his lap and went to the buffet, exaggerating the motions of her hips as she walked. When she finished pouring two glasses of rye whiskey, one considerably fuller than the other, she turned and winked at him.

"I know why you think I invited you here, Mr.

Green." She paused, giggling. "And you're so right. But there's another reason."

"Now, Mommy," he laughed, "who do you think you're kidding? For you there's never any other reason."

"Shame on you." She pretended to be hurt. "How can you say such a thing?"

They laughed together and she handed him the full glass. They clinked rims and drank.

"And now, Mr. Know-It-All," she said. "I'll show you a thing or two."

"There's only one thing you can show me, Mommy. And the sooner the better—"

He tried to pinch her hip, but she dodged his grasp and went to the end table. She searched through the pile of film magazines until she found a particular one.

"I have an announcement to make," she said.

"Let's not get serious. Save it for later."

"No, Bud, I want to show you now. How would you like to look at ninety-six thousand dollars?"

He laughed. "I thought we were supposed to be serious."

"And I am." She opened the magazine and displayed three thick, printed forms. "I want you to take a look at these."

One at a time, she handed him the insurance policies. First the thousand-dollar policy, then the five-thousand-dollar policy and finally, with an appropriately dramatic flourish, the forty-five-thousand-dollar policy.

"And now what do you think of your little business woman?" she said. "Have you noticed that each one is properly signed?"

She watched, smiling, as he examined each policy, his features very sober, his gray eyes puzzled.

She took back the forty-five-thousand-dollar one, waving it in the air.

"I'm proud of this little beauty," she said. "Double indemnity. Ninety thousand."

"Good Lord!" He shook his head slowly from side to side, then gulped his drink. "What does Norman wan

50

with so many policies? I thought you said he didn't give a rap about you and Eileen."

"The Governor? Why he doesn't even know about them."

"Doesn't know about them? Impossible. He signed them, didn't he?"

"Of course he did!" She clapped her hands together gleefully. "Aren't you proud of me? He thought he was signing just that little-bitty, thousand-dollar one. I told him the other two were duplicate copies and he went right ahead and signed them, too. Good old Norman!"

Returning to the buffet, she refilled Ward's glass and handed it to him. He drained half of it and then gazed at her, his eyes even more puzzled.

"I don't believe it," he said. "Nobody would do such a darn foolish thing."

"You don't know the Governor. Busy with his damn car, busy with his damn boat and his sketches, too busy for business. And he admits himself that he's no businessman. That's the one good thing I can say about him. He gives me eighty-five dollars a week to run the house, twice as much as I need. I'll pay the premiums out of that and still have plenty left for my other bills, including you." Pinching his cheek, she kissed him hard on the lips and rumpled his hair.

"I'm sorry about those loans," he said. "I'll start paying you back as soon as business gets better. The trouble is—"

"I know what the trouble is, darling, so you don't have to tell me."

"But I do want to pay you back. The trouble is that I'm losing all those sales on Monday, Wednesday and Friday afternoons, and sometimes I don't feel like going out in the evening and trying to make up a few sales. I feel like—" He paused, then finished with a grin. "Hell, Mommy, half the time after you leave I don't even feel like going out for dinner on those nights."

"I know, darling, I know, but don't you see that—"

"Let me finish," he said. "I know I should stay away

51

from you, Alma. These trips here, three times a week, and all this drinking—I ought to let up for a while. I ought to get back to business and make that two-week swing through Pennsylvania, the way I should have last month—"

"Well, I like that!" she exclaimed. "And leave me sitting around like a dried-up old maid? If you think you'll get away with something like that, you're off your rocker, buster! I'm going with you on that trip, buster!"

She glared at him hotly. She always knew what to do when he began to talk like this. Taking his hands, she pulled him up from his chair and then pressed his palms to her breasts. She leaned forward, moving her shoulders, wriggling against him. When he backed away, she pursued him, still wriggling and when he opened his mouth and licked his lips, she knew she had this small victory half won.

"Damn you," he said. "I ought to have more sense, but every time you start jumping around and rubbing yourself against me I guess I go a little crazy. I ought to—"

"Shut up and listen to me." she said. "Forget about all those little worries of yours. Forget about the loans and the lost sales and the fact that business is lousy and all that small stuff. My God, Bud, don't you realize that when the Governor's gone we'll be able to live the way we want, go to the Waldorf, rent drawing rooms on the train, have a party every night—"

"Wait a minute!" He raised his hand, gesturing for her to be silent. "When the Governor's gone? What the hell are you talking about?"

"I'll give you two guesses, sweetheart. What do you think I'm talking about?"

Reaching around his neck, she clasped her fingers together. She tried to hold him, but he tilted his back sharply, breaking her grip.

He backed away from her, his gray eyes deeply disturbed.

"Alma, don't ever say things like that! Don't you know

52

what it means to even think things like that? Eternal damnation and worse. Eternal—"

"Oh, be quiet," she said impatiently. "I'm not just thinking about it. I'm going to do it! And what's more I've already tried!"

"You what?"

"Yes, lover boy, I've already tried!"

Too late she realized she had gone too far, said too much. His gasp and the pale spots which appeared suddenly on his cheeks warned her to retreat, to say something which would turn the whole thing into a joke or at least a partial joke.

But her mind, which had been turning and twisting so brilliantly, deserted her, frozen when she needed it most. Unable to think of another thing to say, she watched, fascinated, as he backed away from her, a large blue vein bulging at the side of his forehead, his eyes never leaving her face.

"What did you do?" he demanded. "Tell me!"

"I didn't! Bud, I didn't!" Again she groped for the right word, the right phrase, but none came. "I lied to you! I didn't—"

"You did! I can tell by your face! You bitch—you crazy bitch! What did you do?"

For a moment there was silence in the room while he stared at her, waiting for her answer, and she stared back, unable to think of one.

Then he turned and with short, abrupt movements went to the buffet and poured himself a drink. She watched him down it, pour another and drink it just as rapidly, amber beads of liquor shining as they fell from his lips to his shirt front.

"I'll give you—" He wiped the droplets from his mouth. "Alma, I'll give you one more chance to tell me the truth. What did you try to do to him?"

"Nothing. Believe me, Bud, I didn't do a thing!"

"You're lying!"

"I'm not, Bud. Honest!" She went to him, tried to embrace him, but was rebuffed. "Please, Bud, I—"

53

He put on his coat. Twice he tried to button his collar and twice his fumbling fingers failed, but when she tried to help him he thrust her aside. He picked up his leather sample case and started toward the door.

"Bud, don't leave!" Seizing his arm, she tried to keep him from going, but he shook her off.

"Get out of my way!"

"But, Bud, what about our party?"

"To hell with the party!"

"Bud, please stay! I didn't mean what I said. Honest! And I'll make it up to you! We'll have a wonderful party! The best ever, because I'll—"

She almost succeeded in locking her arms around him, but he escaped through the front door.

Safe on the porch, because it was in full view of the neighbors' windows, he halted and looked back at her. His face was pale, almost bloodless-looking, and his hands nervously clasped and unclasped the handle of his leather case.

"Alma, I meant it. I think you're—" He hesitated, then finished in a rush of words. "I think you're crazy!"

"But, Bud, listen to me! Please—"

As soon as she stepped toward him, he turned, fled down the porch steps and out to the sidewalk.

Even when he was half a block away at the intersection of Willard Street, even then he did not look back.

chapter 6

The mornings were always the worst for Ward. Those on the road, when he awoke in unfamiliar hotel rooms, were dreary enough, but the bad taste in his mouth, the aches in bone and muscle were always helped by a swallow or two of rye. Here at home the situation was always twice as dreary and it never improved. There was no way to hide a bottle near the bed, because his wife Virginia snooped and found it every time and poured it down the toilet.

So all he could do was lie here under the blankets, cold and aching, suffering, the taste of his tongue foul and evil, trying to find strength somewhere to rise and face the terrible morning.

For the second time in five minutes, Virginia dashed into the bedroom, thumping his back, screaming at him with that voice of hers which could peel paint at six paces.

"Ward Green, I'm warning you!" She put her mouth so close to his ear his nerves vibrated into the deepest centers of his brain, trebling his agony.

Covering his ears with his hands, he waited for her to finish, but he made the mistake of taking his palms away too soon and caught a fresh blast of words.

"Listen to me, you drunken bum! The Special leaves in just—"

Again he blotted out her shrill cries. Through one partially open eye he watched her rush about the bedroom, brushing her hair, fastening her dress. Then she hurried into the hall, rapping on the door of their daughter's bedroom. He knew it would take considerable time to get Josie up and dressed for wherever the three of them were supposed to go this morning. Josie, who was ten, was at that stage where she wanted to dress well and look nice. He was sure he could remain here, recuperating slowly, for at least ten more minutes while Josie hunted up her hair ribbon or her stockings or her belt or something else that was always getting lost.

Now he heard Virginia clattering in the kitchen as she prepared breakfast, shouting at him to get up, making far more noise than was necessary.

Drawing the blankets tighter around him, he turned his face to the wall and tried to doze. But it was impossible. Josie was in the bathroom now, running water noisily. *Oh, God*, he thought, *if only they would go away and let me remain here all day to regain my strength*. He felt weak and sick and it was in this condition that the guilt always weighed the heaviest, forcing itself upon him, making him weaker and sicker. And more ashamed of himself.

"Ward Green!" his wife shouted. "I'm warning you! The Special leaves in twenty-five minutes!"

The Special? He tried to think about the Special, hoping it would draw his mind out from under its pressing guilt. Why were they going to take the Special? Where were they supposed to go this morning?

"And the flowers, too!" Virginia shouted. "We've got to pick them up before we get on the Special!"

He groaned and felt like throwing up. Now he remembered. The damn Special to the cemetery. The streetcar that left so damned early. What time did it leave? He racked his brain, trying to make its cells perform, trying to keep it from dwelling on his guilt and shame. Eight o'clock, wasn't that it? So damnably early. And what day was this? He forced himself to think. Memorial Day, that was it. But what year? He forced himself to think harder. May 30, 1926, of course.

He started to congratulate himself on his clear thinking. And then, abruptly, it was all a mistake. Because he remembered last year, last Memorial Day, and what a pleasant day the three of them had enjoyed in the country after visiting the cemetery. Virginia, Josie and himself, picnicking near the river, fashioning yellow garlands from dandelions and tossing them into the stream.

He rubbed his eyes, rubbed hard, trying to shut out the images. Was it only a year ago that they had been such a well-adjusted little family? He knew the answer too well. It had been only half a dozen days later, June 6 to be exact, that he'd met Alma. And that had been the beginning of everything.

And now he was really sick. Now his belly boiled with nausea like a cauldron. Now the guilt was on him like a great marble stone, a tombstone. *Thou Shall Not Commit Adultery. Thou Shalt Not Covet Thy Neighbor's wife.* Alma and her body. Alma and her yellow garters. Alma on beds in a dozen different hotel rooms, Alma on a double bed, Alma on a twin bed, Alma on a sofa. He groaned and rubbed his stomach. Why had he gone to Truzzillini's for lunch that day in June? Why hadn't he gone to some other restaurant? But Ralph had insisted. And they hadn't been seated there five minutes before Ralph spotted two friends at a table under the arch. Two girl friends. Alma and another woman. Mame somebody. Oh, God, if only he hadn't gone to Truzzillini's.

"Out!" Virginia's voice went off in his ear like a bomb. "Get out of that bed!"

This time he had failed to hear her come in and before he could prevent her she seized his arm and rolled him off the bed to the floor. The impact made his head ring with pain.

"Get in the tub!" She poked him with her foot. "Wash that stink off you! That stinking stuff you drink! Hurry now, I'm warning you!"

Rising from the floor, he stumbled off to the sanctuary of the bathroom where he might steal a few more minutes of rest. Josie, coming out, met him at the door and gave him a nervous half-smile which told him that she knew all about the condition he'd been in when he came home long after midnight.

He wanted to vomit but he did not have enough strength. For a minute, two minutes, he rested on the toilet while the bathtub filled with water. When he sat in the tub, he cursed because the water wasn't even lukewarm. It was another of Virginia's many ways of reminding him of their unpaid bills. To keep the fuel bill down, she turned the water heater flame so low there was only hot water enough for half a tub and Josie had used all of it.

When he shaved, also with cold water, he gashed himself in the difficult whisker area beneath his left nostril. Dressed finally in his gray suit, white shirt, and wine-colored tie, he desperately needed several cups of coffee, but Virginia refused to let him take time even for one.

Out the door the three of them went, hurrying along the sidewalk at a pace which made his head ache and his stomach churn. At McNaughton's Market, two blocks away, they made a quick stop for seventy-five cents' worth of white carnations and when he looked into his wallet he was surprised that he had only six dollars left from the most recent twenty Alma had given him. It was after eight when they arrived at the streetcar stop, but fortunately the Special was late and by running the last twenty steps they got aboard just before the long, bile-green car got under way.

All during the six-mile ride he was miserable, his stomach buffeted by the irregular motions of the heavy wheels directly beneath their seat, his head in agony from the continual shrieking of the steel brakes as they made stop after stop. When he tried to doze, Virginia poked him with her elbow, making him sit upright.

He pitied himself, thinking how changed she was, how different from the Virginia of last year, how sharply she spoke to him, how rudely she pushed him. At thirty-three, she was still a fairly good-looking woman, but definitely not in Alma's class. She was as tall as he, slightly taller than Alma, thinner—a brunette with small breasts and flat hips, a rather sexless woman. They had, in fact, stopped having sexual relations for a long time before he met Alma. Virginia had very little interest in sex and that was undoubtedly why she never suspected him of having an affair with another woman. For Virginia, sex was a chore, like rinsing the milk bottles and cleaning out the sink. There had never been any joy in their love-making and Virginia had never—not once in the dozen years of their marriage—indicated that she was impressed by his masculinity.

They put most of the white carnations on the double grave of Virginia's mother and father, who had died in the flu epidemic of 1918. The few blossoms left, less than a half dozen, went into a sun-frosted jar on the grave of Ward's father. As he replaced the container, he tried to think of a phrase from the Bible, something appropriate to murmur, but he couldn't think of anything. Well, it didn't matter much. He hadn't known his father very well. His parents had been divorced when he was small and he had been raised by his mother. His father, who had never been strong, had died when Ward was thirteen, and even after he was gone his mother never had a good word to say about the old man. Until Ward's marriage to Virginia, the grave had gone flowerless year after year.

Their duties at the cemetery completed, they walked across the street to Grant Park and selected a grassy site beneath two elms for their picnic tablecloth. Virginia always chose this spot and for a while she stopped criticizing him, content to play games with Josie. He welcomed the chance to rest, making a pillow of his coat, choosing a spot where the rays of the late morning sun could soothe his tired muscles. Half awake, half asleep, he thought about his mother and how she was spending the holiday alone in her room in the boarding house. It was a shame that he and Virginia couldn't take her somewhere today, but he had learned long ago that it was useless to ask Virginia to do things for his mother. His mother had always been good to him, and it was a shame that he couldn't do more for her. His mother was one of the two people in his life who made him feel wanted and useful. The other person, of course, was Alma.

Like a celluloid ball bobbing about a whirlpool, his mind toyed with thoughts of Alma, tried to avoid thinking about her, and then was sucked in. He remembered last afternoon and evening, how she'd worn only the yellow garters, nothing else, not even stockings. Twice she had removed her clothes. Twice she had forced him to display energy which he did not think he possessed. It had been excruciating but exciting. No matter what Alma did, it was always exciting. Again and again he had tried to break with her, not see her any more, and each time he returned, finding her even more desirable. She was like a fever in his blood. It was all wrong, but there was no changing things—not while the thought of her loveliness and wantonness was a fierce torment, an almost evil obsession.

Licking the dry roof of his mouth and his drier lips, he wished he had something to drink. Even beer. Thoughts of Alma always made him feel dry, made his mouth feel strange. In so many ways she was a feline woman, stealthy and secret. There were times when she said terrible things and displayed terrible facial expressions which made him fear her. Like last November.

When he'd left her house after that stormy lunch scene, he'd sworn to himself that he would never see her again. His stern resolution had lasted not quite five days. And after the new and more violent passion of their love-making, he'd forced himself to ask her again about those things she'd hinted at previously, the things she'd been doing to her husband. Willingly she'd told him, her large blue-green eyes glistening with hatred for Norman. It was difficult to tell when she was lying, making up fantasies, and when she was telling the truth. With oaths and excited gestures, she'd boasted about how she'd closed the garage doors, hoping he'd suffocate on the exhaust fumes. She'd also boasted of other plans which had failed, like the time she'd kicked loose the gas heater hose near the sofa and almost asphyxiated Norman. And there was also her crazy story about the medicine for Norman's hiccoughs. She had bottles and bottles of medicines. She told her family, of course, that she was making continual visits to the doctor on Mondays, Wednesdays and Fridays, and buying medicines for her alleged anemia. She said she'd dosed Norman for two weeks with iron tonic spiked with bichloride of mercury. Heaven only knew where she had obtained the poison. But it hadn't worked. She claimed that Norman hadn't even felt ill after the doses. Instead, the damn stuff had cleared up Norman's hiccoughs completely.

Closing his eyes tight, he tried to stop thinking about her. There was no really good reason why he shouldn't break with her once and for all. All it took was a display of will power, like trying to sell a customer four dozen corselets when all he needed was three dozen. There was no doubt in his mind that things could not be allowed to continue the way they were. He was deeper in debt than ever. Some days he was able to make up for the lost sales, the lost accounts, but there were other times when he was too tired to make the extra trips and put on the extra pressure that a big sale required.

He rolled over on his back and let the sunlight warm his face and chest. He would put a stop to it. As of today, as of last night, he was through with her. Twice in one evening was too much and even then she wasn't satisfied. If he didn't stop seeing her, there was no telling what might happen. And the continual drinking was just as bad for him, and expensive, too. Half the money she gave him went for drugstore booze.

Sitting up, he leaned against the cool trunk of one of the elms and gazed at Virginia and Josie who held paper plates in their laps.

"I asked you before," Virginia said. "Do you want some of this chicken or don't you?"

He shook his head. He'd been so deep in thought he hadn't heard Virginia's words.

"I'm thirsty," he said.

"Then have some milk."

The thought of milk made his stomach squeeze together like a sponge.

"I'd rather have water," he said.

He followed a sandy path through the trees and up a slope to where the rest rooms and a drinking fountain were located. The water tasted sulphurous and he drank very little. He sat by himself on a green bench in the sun, enjoying his solitude until he noticed a man coming up the path with a decidedly wobbly walk. The man was elderly, in his seventies at least, his cheeks marred with the tiny broken red veins of the alcoholic. In his coat pocket was the undeniable bulge of a bottle.

Ward rose and followed the old man into the men's room. Halting near one of the open stalls, the man drew the bottle out—it looked like gin—and drank.

"I was wondering—" Ward paused, one part of his mind surprised that he should be reduced to such pleading tones, while another part of his mind indicated it was no longer surprised at the things he did.

"I was wondering," he said again, "if I could have a sip."

The old man lowered the bottle, brushed his tongue across brown, ugly teeth and drew air wetly into his nostrils.

"It'll cost you, mister."

"How much?"

"Fifty."

Ward drew the coin from his pocket and handed it over. He put the warm bottle top to his lips and drank fast, letting the gin run down his throat so rapidly it burned like acid. The old man reached for the bottle, but Ward turned quickly away, managing another good swallow before the man pulled it from his mouth.

"Damn you!" the old man said. "You damn near killed it!"

Pleased with himself, Ward grinned at the old man's irritation and discomfort.

He walked back outside and seated himself on the green bench in the sunlight. He felt the liquor moving slowly within him, warming him, seeping into the lower parts of his stomach. He leaned his head back and began to think about Alma. There was no reason to break off with Alma right away. Later maybe, but not right away. Those things she said she did to her husband shouldn't be considered too seriously. Fantasies, no doubt. Fantasies from all the bad movies she saw and all the magazines she read.

He thought about her yellow garters and the circular marks that remained on her legs after the garters were removed.

"I'll phone her," he said aloud, pleased with the authoritative sound of his voice. "As soon as we get home this evening. God damn it, I'll phone her from McNaughton's Market."

chapter 7

Alma sat before her vanity mirror, making up her face. It was early March, a stormy, snowy day, but nevertheless she felt certain that her months of strategy, her months of patience and persistence, were close to bringing results. Within her now was the strong feeling that she could direct him into any unfamiliar channel she chose, so long as she acted firmly and with confidence.

There would be failures, of course, little withdrawals on his part, even anger and outright rebellion at times. And she was bound to make mistakes herself, occasionally; she knew quite well that she was no brain, no genius, so the main thing was confidence, lots of confidence in herself. And if she slipped, if she made errors, there was always her most powerful weapon to fall back on, the one weapon he was never able to resist. Unless, of course, he was too stupified with drink or too exhausted—and those effects certainly didn't come under the heading of resistance.

She had made what she considered the final test in Baltimore, where they had spent the previous weekend.

When she'd originally started lending him money, he had protested first, then accepted. But last Saturday night when she offered him the whole three hundred dollars—money saved carefully out of her weekly allotments from Norman, he had not made even the meekest protest. Nor had he protested when she talked about how she hated Norman and how she planned to give him a sleeping powder and then hit him on the head with a heavy hammer.

It had been really quite astonishing. She had talked on and on about Norman, telling how easy it would be to approach him at night because he rarely awoke after going to bed and he always slept on his good ear. As a result, because he was nearly deaf in his left ear, he always slept soundly. All the time she talked, Ward had merely sat at the table, staring at her sleepily, nodding or shaking his head, finishing the bottle of rye and then asking politely if she'd brought another. She had, of course, and when she drew it from her purse, he thanked her and went on drinking, nodding his head at her, commenting when necessary. No matter how drunk he was, he never looked really drunk. He never became upset or unruly. Even after several hours of steady drinking, his voice didn't become badly slurred. The only way you could be sure he was drunk was to study the color of his face. When he was quite drunk, his face and neck were thoroughly red. But when he was very, very drunk, his face became pale except for dollar-sized spots of red on his cleft chin and on his cheeks.

As she strapped on her golden wrist watch, she noted the time. Twelve-thirty. Just about time for the taxi to arrive.

"Eileen!" she called. "Are you about ready?"

"Yes, Mama." Eileen spoke from the other room where she was dressing.

"Don't dawdle."

"No, Mama."

Carefully Alma drew her hat, a pink cloche, down over her newly marcelled hair, arranging the brim at the correct angle above her eyebrows. After adding more coral color to her lips, she was satisfied with her image in the vanity mirror, but she did not rise. She remained seated before the mirror for an additional moment, admiring her appearance, thinking again about Bud's remarkable statement last Saturday night.

She hadn't been at all certain that he had been listening to the rambling details of her plan to strike Norman on the head while he was asleep.

But then, out of the blue, Bud had spoken.

"Don't use a hammer," he said. "Use something else. Something heavier. Maybe a sash weight."

And that was it. That was the turning point. For the first time, he had made a suggestion. For the first time he had showed a willingness to participate. And he had even gone a remarkable step further. When he had started to make love to her, rather clumsily because he was so drunk, she had put him off.

"Later," she'd said. "First I want you to try something for me."

"What?"

"These powders." She'd opened her purse and showed him the small white envelopes. "I want you to see if they work. Will you do that for me, darling?"

Without a single protest, he had agreed. He had shaken half the contents of one envelope into his glass and then poured in a good amount of rye. He had winked at her as he drank it, trying to look roguish, trying to look very masculine and self-confident. Almost immediately he had fallen into a deep sleep.

He had slept from ten o'clock that night until noon on Sunday. Fourteen hours. And when he awoke—my, what a change. She smiled to herself, remembering how good he'd been. It had been one of their best parties. Every bit as good as some of the parties she'd had with Scotty or Ralph. And far, far better than anything Norman had ever done.

Outside the house, the taxi's horn sounded. She buttoned her gray Persian lamb coat to the neck, because it would be cold out, and went into the hall where Eileen was waiting, wearing galoshes, mittens and overcoat. It was too bad Eileen had to tag along today, but it couldn't be helped. With Mrs. Jansson away baby-sitting, it wouldn't be right to leave Eileen home nursing the cold that had kept her out of school today. Besides, with Norman so cranky and unreasonable lately, it might be well to have Eileen along to back up her story of how they had spent the afternoon.

It was snowing more heavily when they dashed from the house to the red taxi and Alma swore when she snagged her stocking on the high, square running board.

"Oh, Mama," Eileen scolded, "you said a bad word."

"I'm sorry, dear. I couldn't help it."

"You shouldn't have, should you?"

"No, dear."

"Do you know what Daddy says?" Eileen persisted. "He says ladies who swear are bad."

"And they are, dear. Most of them."

"Are you going to buy me something today, Mama?"

"Maybe."

"You really should."

"Why should I?"

"So I won't tell Daddy."

"Tell Daddy what?"

Alma looked sharply at her daughter. At times Eileen seemed far more aware of things than a nine-year-old should.

"That you said a bad word," Eileen replied.

"Oh, that." Alma relaxed against the taxi cushions. "You needn't bother telling him that. Besides, didn't I tell you what you can have for desert today?"

"What?"

"A double chocolate sundae!"

"A double? Really? With slivered almonds?"

"Yes, with slivered almonds."

With that problem solved, the remainder of the ride to Truzzillini's was uneventful. Inside the restaurant, the head waiter, a tall Italian with sparkling brown eyes, led them to a table in the alcove where Bud was waiting.

She noted at once that Bud's cheeks and neck were pink, meaning that he was pretty well along, even though it was scarcely one o'clock.

Politely he rose from his chair, remaining standing until they were seated.

"And how are you today, Eileen?" he asked.

"Sick," she said, wiping her nose daintily with a small lace handkerchief.

"She's got a cold," Alma said.

"Sorry to hear that," Bud said. "And how are you, Mommy?"

Scarcely before the word was out of his mouth, Eileen giggled and turned to her mother.

"Did you hear what he called you?"

"It was nothing," Alma said calmly. "A slip of the tongue."

"Yes," said Bud. "A slip of the tongue."

He tried very hard to pass it off lightly, but his cheeks had become pale, and for the next few minutes his hand shook noticeably as he toyed with his fork and spoon. They ordered veal scallopini with mushrooms and spaghetti, small green salads and coffee. During the meal Alma and Eileen chatted about books, tests, teachers and other trivia of school. Bud added little to the conversation. Midway through the entree he excused himself and went to the men's room. When he returned he walked quite steadily, but there was a distinct odor of rye whiskey on his breath which Alma hoped Eileen wouldn't notice.

She waited until the large chocolate sundae was placed before Eileen. Then, while the little girl was happily occupied with her spoon, Alma drew from her purse a wrinkled envelope and wrote several words on the back of it with a pencil.

She turned the envelope around so he could read the question: *Did you bring the chloroform?*

He shook his head.

Frowning, she wrote another question: *Did you bring the other things?*

His eyes did not meet hers. He looked down at his clasped hands and shook his head.

"The nerve of you!" she said.

Shredding the envelope, she threw the pieces angrily onto the table. The more she thought about his deliberate disobedience, his defiance, the angrier sb became.

"Who do you think you are!" sh exclaimed. "You weak little, puny little—"

She stopped herself in ti , before the scene got out of hand. Snapping her se shut, she pushed her chair back and rose quickly ner feet.

"Come, Eileen!"

She took the c ild's reluctant hand and pulled her away from the table.

"But, Mama! I'm not finished! My sundae, Mama! I'm—"

Eileen cried and dragged her feet across the entire length of the fashionable dining room. She did not stop caterwauling until Alma struck her once, smartly, across the cheek. Then, stunned into silence, she stared at her mother and followed close at her heels as they finished their march into the vestibule. At the doorway Alma stopped, looking back over her shoulder.

He was still at the table, sitting rigidly, mopping his forehead and glasses with a napkin.

She let him suffer for a week.

During that time, she would not talk to him on the phone, nor did she show up at the hotel on Wednesday or Friday afternoon. She did not answer his notes, two of them on successive days, begging her to meet him, promising to bring the things she had asked for.

On Sunday, while Norman was out in the garage tinkering with the Essex, she consented to talk to Bud for a minute on the phone. He was in a state of extreme nervousness, very meek during the first part of the conversation and very excited during the last part when she promised to meet him Monday afternoon.

"Remember," she warned, "if you don't bring the things, I'll leave again, just like last week."

"I'll bring them!" His voice was almost shrill in the receiver. "I'll be there, Mommy! It's been hell all week, thinking about you, wondering when you'd let me see you—"

There was no telling how long he would have carried on like that, beseeching her, imploring her.

"All right," she said softly, before hanging up. "Three o'clock. Truzzillini's."

She arrived half an hour late, alone this time because Eileen was in school and would have supper at a chum's house. He was waiting for her at the same table in the alcove and he was in approximately the same state of drunkenness, cheeks pink, his forehead shining with perspiration despite the coldness of the day. He was twice as nervous as before, his hands straying to the initialed stickpin on his necktie, to the silverware, to the buttons on his vest.

"Did you bring the things?" she asked.

"Yes."

"The chloroform?" She kept her voice low so the waiter could not overhear.

"Yes."

"The sash weight?"

"Yes."

"The gloves, the handkerchiefs and the rope?"

"Yes. Everything except the rope."

"What happened to the rope?"

He bit his lip nervously. "I forgot it. But I'll get some."

"Where are the things?"

"Here." He pushed the tablecloth aside so she could see the two brown-paper parcels on the chair beside him. "Can we go to the hotel now?"

"No. We have some other things to talk about first. And I want a piece of pie."

His nervousness increased while she sipped her coffee and consumed delicate forkfuls of butter-pecan pie topped with whipped cream. She smiled at him, but did not let him know it was a smile of triumph. She had been certain her most powerful weapon would not fail her, and it had succeeded better than she'd planned. He was positively jumping all over the place, unable to sit still on his chair for more than a few seconds at a time.

"Please, Mommy." His eyes looked at her imploringly. "Can't we go to the hotel now? You have no idea what I've been through all week, wondering, waiting."

"In a few minutes. First we have a few things to settle."

"Can't that wait? Can't we—"

"No, Bud, it can't. You'll come out to the house *this* Friday night, is that clear?"

"I suppose so."

"Nine o'clock, understand?"

"Yes."

"You *will* have the rope?"

"Yes." Miserably, he gazed down at his fingers which were folding and unfolding a napkin. "Can't we go to the hotel now?"

"No. You'll wait outside, on the sidewalk. I'll try to give the Governor one of the sleeping powders, and if he's asleep I'll turn on the lamp in Mother's room. That will mean you can come upstairs, do you understand?"

"I guess so."

"You needn't worry about mother. She'll be away for the night baby-sitting. Do you have any questions?"

"No."

Finishing her coffee, she placed the cup quietly on its saucer. "I guess that's all. I suppose we can go now."

At once he stood up and beckoned to the waiter.

"Finally!" he whispered hoarsely. "My God, Alma, how much of this do you think a man can stand?"

She arrived home at five, earlier than usual because Bud had been too excited and nervous to perform well at the hotel. By the time she carried the five-pound sash weight and the other package down the cellar stairs, her

71

arms and wrists were aching. She buried both bundles in the powdery ashes in one of the metal barrels behind the furnace.

When she went upstairs to the kitchen, she was surprised to see Norman seated at the table eating graham crackers and drinking a bottle of lemon soda pop. He was home at least a half-hour early.

"What kind of a place is this?" he grumbled. "Man comes in hungry, needing something to eat after working all day, and there's nobody home. Where the hell is everybody?"

She threw her coat over one of the wooden chairs and opened the ice box.

"Mama's baby-sitting," she said. "Eileen's having supper at Ruthie Heinrich's. I'll have something on the table in a few minutes."

"Beans and sausage, I'll bet," he said sourly. "That's all you ever fix."

"Wrong as usual," she lied. Putting the sausages back on the ice, she took out a package of corned beef and a bowl of two-day-old boiled potatoes.

"Leftovers," he said. "You can bet your sweet life Winifred wouldn't fix a hungry man leftovers. She'd have something good on the table right this minute, like steak and—"

"Don't bring that woman up again," she said. "I'm doing the best I can. Why didn't you tell me you'd be home early?"

"Winifred wouldn't bellyache all the time," he said. "Winifred would stay home and plan a fine dinner—"

"Oh, shut up," she said. "If you mention that woman's name again, you can fix your own damn dinner!"

Hands on her hips, she turned from the range and glared at him. She knew he was provoking her deliberately, as he always did when he thought he had found an advantage.

He crossed his long legs and folded his arms across his heavy, muscular chest. He let his face, tanned and weathered from countless weekends of boating and fishing, display an expression of piety and devotion to the memory of his dearly deceased fiancée.

"She was not a woman." He tried to make his rough voice soft and gentle, but succeeding only in sounding foolish. "She was a young fraulein, sweet and unspoiled, just a girl. And she was better than you in a dozen ways, better-looking, better—"

"Shut up!" Alma said. "If you think I'm going to stand here and listen—"

Ignoring her protests, his voice went on and on, his brown eyes looking at her with contempt and scorn. "She would have made me a better wife than you, far better. She would have given me fine sons by now, two or three sons, instead of that spoiled brat of a girl you gave me!"

"Oh, shut up! If you loved her so much, why did you ever marry me? The way you chased me, the things you said to me on the telephone! There I was, barely nineteen, innocent, knowing nothing, a fourteen-dollar-a-week phone operator. And you, thirty-two already, an editor, knowing everything—how you tried to sweet-talk me into it! You were disgusting! That was the only reason you married me, because that was all you wanted from me, and that was the only way you could get it!"

She dumped the corned beef and potatoes from the frying pan onto his plate.

"Now eat that!" She pushed the plate in front of him. "Eat that and shut up, you Heinie pig!"

His eyes grew cold with anger.

"What did you call me?"

"Pig!" She snapped the word, enjoying the bitter, angry taste of it. "A Heinie pig! And who do you think you're fooling the way you spell your name? Norman Chrysler." She started to spell it out. "C-H-R—"

"Shut up!" His heavy fist struck the table so hard his fork tumbled to the floor. "I'm warning you, Alma! Shut up!"

73

"C-H-R-Y-S-L-E-R!" she spelled, tauntingly. "It looks so dignified. But people know you're a Heinie pig! People know your name is really Norman Hans Kreisler. K-R-E-I-S-L-E-R! They know you changed it during the war, you Heinie coward!"

"Alma, shut up!" He erupted from his chair, upsetting it on the floor.

"And that isn't all they know!" she taunted. "They know where you go on Saturday nights when you're supposed to be bowling. They know about that doxie of yours on East Twelfth Street!"

His face was suddenly the same reddish-brown color as the corned beef and when he spoke again his voice was a roar.

"Shut your foul mouth! Bitch! You cheap—"

"Heinie pig!"

As he strode toward her, she said it again and again, knowing that he was going to hit her, wanting him to hit her.

"Heinie pig! Heinie pig!"

His heavy hand caught her full on the cheek, a blow that knocked her sideways against the range. He struck her again, on the same cheek, and she felt two sharp pains at once, burning pains. To escape him, she tumbled to the floor, screaming curses at him, half-expecting him to kick her.

For a long moment his shadow towered above her while he shouted at her, swearing in German and English. Finally he turned and went toward the hallway, his angry footsteps making the floor shake and rattling the pans in the cupboard.

She remained on the floor until long after he stomped from the house. She wept and cursed and wept some more when she saw the burns the range had inflicted on her left palm when she fell against it.

She did not stop weeping until she remembered the two parcels hidden in the ashes in the cellar. Then, feeling better almost instantly, she rose to her feet. Brushing the tears from her eyes with her fingertips, she opened her purse and got out a stick of gum.

"You'll be sorry!" she said.

She chewed the gum viciously, feeling the muscles grow tight and hard in her cheek.

"You'll be sorry, you Heinie bastard!"

chapter 8

It was Friday night. He stood in the office looking at a wall calendar, hoping he was wrong about the date. But it was not Wednesday night or Thursday night. It was definitely Friday night, six o'clock, and in three hours he was due at Alma's house.

He felt very tired. He had eaten part of a bowl of tomato soup for lunch and nothing since then. He knew he should go out and find some dinner, stuff some strength into himself, but he was totally without appetite. His stomach felt thick and useless and he knew he shouldn't pour any more whiskey into it. The whiskey was of such miserable quality that it left a bitter metallic taste in his mouth which nothing would rinse away. And yet, without the whiskey he would be lost, completely lost.

Seating himself at his desk, he finished the bottle and dropped it in the lower drawer with a clutter of order books and sales slips. He pushed the drawer shut with his foot and then he gazed slowly around the dim, deserted office, trying to remember something he was supposed to do tonight. Somewhere else.

Finally his weary mind remembered. The rope. Alma had said bring a piece of rope.

He walked around the other desks, peering into waste-baskets, checking the supply cabinet, examining the shelf above the bookkeeper's filing cabinets. His movements were well controlled, hardly those of a man who had been drinking most of the day. He went through the doorway into the stockroom, switched on the bright bulb overhead, and blinked at the cartons of corsets piled on the floor and on the shelves. There was string on a spindle above the wrapping counter, but it was not what he wanted. He shook his head. Correction: It was not what Alma wanted.

He compromised. A large carton of corsets from the factory was bound with light wire. He removed it. And as his fingers formed the eight-foot length into a coil, he was sure it would not be used for the purpose Alma spoke about. He had given the matter hours and hours of thought. She would not do it, of course. And even if she was foolish enough to try, he would not help her. He would go there, he would talk to her, but he would most certainly not help her.

It was eight-thirty when he got off the bus. It had been threatening rain all day, but now the night was so cold it hinted of snow. As he drew his overcoat lapels closer about his throat, fastening the top button, he felt the coil of wire in the inner breast pocket. He had a strong urge to toss it into the gutter, but he did not. He would do as he promised. He would bring it to her and let her decide what to do with it.

The street in front of the Chrysler house was so dark, the roofs of the houses and the tops of the trees were invisible. It was a few minutes before nine when he paused in front of the house, looking up at the second floor for the lamp signal which Alma was to leave for him. The lamp was supposed to be lit in the bedroom of her mother, who was away baby-sitting.

But there was no light burning anywhere on the second floor. Light glowed behind the living room shades

77

and appeared dimly in the cellar window, but the rest of the house was dark.

He kept walking. He went to the end of the block and returned. There was still no light from any of the bedrooms on the second floor.

He walked and walked. He walked completely around the block, crossed the street and walked around the adjoining block. Part of the time, he walked in a kind of stupor, a mental blankness brought on by all the liquor he'd drunk during the day, the lack of food and his general fatigue. He did very little thinking. There was nothing to be gained from trying to reason out why he was here, walking aimlessly around the neighborhood. Actually it was far better to walk than to contemplate what might happen if he went into the house. He had promised to come and he was here. That was all. The rest was up to her.

When he took his watch from his vest pocket, he was astonished to see that it was nearly eleven o'clock. It didn't seem possible that so much time had elapsed. He walked back toward the house again, but there was still no signal upstairs. The yellow rectangles of light formed by the living room and cellar windows were unchanged.

As he turned away, a light went on in the kitchen and was quickly extinguished. Again it flickered on and off. He decided it might be a signal.

Reluctantly he went up the stone path to the rear of the house. He heard a small tapping sound and saw Alma's face gazing at him whitely through the kitchen window, her finger touching the pane.

Her face vanished and in a moment the kitchen door opened.

"Come inside," she whispered.

As soon as he stepped into the warm, dark kitchen, she embraced him. Caressing his face, his chin and throat, her hands were hot and moist. She kissed him, opening her mouth and sighing softly. Through the thin nightgown he felt her breasts and the curve of her hip.

78

"Oh, Bud," she whispered. "I'm so glad you came."
They kissed again.
"I'm sorry about the signal," she said.
"What happened?"
"He hasn't gone up to bed yet. He's been down in the cellar chopping wood. Exercise, he calls it."
"All this time?"
"Yes. Did you bring the rope?"
Her voice was low, the question intense with meaning.
"No. I—"
"You fool! You promised!" Her fingernails went sharply, angrily, into the flesh of his neck. "What's the matter with you? Why didn't you bring it?"
"I brought some wire," he said. "I—"
"Wire? Oh." She was silent a moment. "It'll work as well, won't it?"
"I suppose so."
"Do you want to go upstairs now, darling? You can wait in Mother's bedroom."
"No."
"Why not?"
"I don't feel good. My stomach's all upset."
"You mean you don't want to do it tonight?"
"No. I'm not up to it tonight, Alma. I—"
He fully expected her to explode with wrath, to curse him and insult him. He swayed against her, closing his eyes, wishing he had something to drink, a long pull of something, anything, even that evil stuff he'd finished back at the office.
"All right, dear," she said. "Not tonight. Some other night soon."
Her mildness astonished him and he was sure then that he had guessed right. She didn't want to do it, either. It was all talk on her part, one of her fantasies.
"Another night," she added. She swore under her breath, but loud enough for him to hear the names she called her husband. "He *would* have to chop wood tonight, of all nights."
He remained in the dark kitchen a few more minutes,

gulping two long drinks from the bottle of bourbon she handed him. Then he opened the door.

"Wait a minute," she said.

She returned almost immediately and pressed another bottle into his hand, a smaller one, its shape familiar.

"The chloroform," she whispered. "Take it with you."

Relief, sweet relief, poured through him. Now he was certain she didn't want to go through with it.

"Thank God," he said. "You're doing the right thing, Alma. We can—"

"Oh, shut up!" she said. "I don't want to risk having him smell the stuff and wonder what it's for." Her fingers pinched his cheek. "Don't think you're getting out of it, because you're not! I'll pick another night!"

For emphasis she pinched his cheek harder, inflicting a sharper pain. "I'll write you a note. Now get out of here before he comes up the stairs and finds us!"

She pushed him out the door and closed it behind him.

He walked slowly along the sidewalk, trying not to think about what she had said. When he was nearly a block away from her house, he leaned against the rough trunk of a tree and fought a silent battle with his stomach, trying to keep from losing the bourbon.

He did not succeed.

She was better than her word. She did not write simply one note. She wrote four letters which were delivered to him on four successive days at four different hotels. Familiar with his sales route through New York and New Jersey, she knew what cities he would visit and how long he would stay in each.

The fourth letter, containing three ten-dollar bills, was waiting when he arrived at the hotel in Syracuse. Despite its deeper implications he was glad to get it. And it was not just because of the money, which he planned to send home to Virginia and Josie. The trip had been going badly, very badly, and he needed something to cheer him up after losing both the Rincon Shops and McNeil Department Store sales, two accounts he'd had for years. As usual, her handwriting was poorly constructed, the words slanting irregularly all' over the pages, and even though there was a threat at the end, the letter made him feel better. When he got upstairs in his room, he read it over again.

My Own Lover Boy:
    Gee, but I'm happy. Oh, but I'm happy, thinking about Sat. night and how swell everything's going to be after that. All I keep thinking of is you, you darn lovable little cuss. I could eatcha all up. Could I get lit & put out this blaze that's so much bother to me? Ah yes—hon. After Sat. night, we'll put it out, both of us, and get good and plastered—isn't that a nice word? Beginning to think I'm already that way on nothing. Hurry home, darling, I'll be waiting for you.
All my love,
YOUR MOMMY
P. S. If you're not here, you'll know what will happen, don't you?

Thursday night she phoned him at the hotel and as soon as he heard her voice, full of love and desire, he knew that no matter what she did or said, he needed her more than he had ever needed anyone in his life.

"What time will you get in Saturday?" she asked.

"Around eleven or so."

"Make it midnight," she said. "It'll probably be one A.M. or so before we get back from the Dockstaders. You'll be sure and bring the things, won't you? Especially the gloves, so it will look like burglary."

"Yes."

"If everything's all right, I'll leave the cigarettes out on the table. And I'll leave the other things for you in Mother's room, under the pillow. And you be sure and set up an alibi, won't you?"

"An alibi?"

"Certainly, darling. We don't want anyone to know you're going to be here, do we?"

"No, I guess not."

"All right, hon. And, remember, the kitchen door will be unlocked. And you know what will happen if you don't come, don't you?"

"Yes."

"Good-by until Saturday, hon. And don't forget I love you—and that we'll get good and plastered afterward. I love you very much, sweet."

"And I love you, Mommy."

As soon as they hung up, he started drinking and he stayed in the room all of the next day, Friday, drinking, giving most of his money to a bell captain who brought him overpriced bottles of rye. Within him, hour after hour, developed the fear that this time Alma really meant to do something terrible. Half a dozen times he told himself he would not show up Saturday night, yet each time he said it he knew he would. He could not understand what was wrong with him. Despite all the liquor, he had slept badly each night on the trip. He was tired, exhausted, mentally wrung out, and in the last few weeks he'd lost another five pounds, weight he could not afford to lose. And yet he had an enormous desire to be with her, to touch her, to feel her body, to see her lying there with that expression of pure lust on her face. If he did not go he would lose her, there could be no doubt about that. And if he lost her he would be lost himself, completely, totally, because he had to have her.

It was raining Saturday night when he walked slowly up the sidewalk toward the dark Chrysler house. It was pouring heavily, cold rain which soaked his leather sample case and dripped from the brim of his hat.

He stood out front for nearly five minutes, shivering, debating whether to go in, rubbing his mouth as he remembered Alma's promise to leave him a bottle. A sudden gale swept down the street, driving heavy drops of water into his face, and he fled before it to the safety of the house, dashing in through the unlocked kitchen door.

Before he could close it, the wind tore the door from his grasp, slamming it shut with an explosion which reverberated through the darkened house. He stood rigidly, feeling his heart hurtling itself against his ribs, listening for sounds that would mean someone else was astir in the house.

He heard nothing except the drip-drip of rainwater falling from his overcoat to the floor.

Cautiously he walked to the kitchen table. In the darkness he could not find the package of cigarettes she was supposed to leave as a sign. He hunted over almost all of the wooden surface with both gloved hands. When he found the package he became confused, unable to remember whether the cigarettes meant he was to go upstairs or remain here. He licked his lips and tried to swallow. He needed a drink so badly he decided to take his chances upstairs.

Even after he found his way safely to the correct bedroom—Mrs. Jansson's—his heart continued to beat rapidly. He went straight to the bed and put his hands underneath the pillow. His gloved fingers encountered the heavy sash weight and recoiled nervously. He found other objects—another pair of gloves, some cotton waste, and, finally, the bottle. It was only a pint but it was good quality bourbon, far better than the watered stuff the bell captain had supplied him with at the hotel. Sitting on the bed he had three quick pulls on the bottle and then, feeling somewhat better, he removed his wet coat and hat and hung them in Mrs. Jansson's closet.

He opened his sample case and removed the coil of wire, the bottle of chloroform and the Italian newspaper he'd bought on the train. He put those objects under the pillow with the others and then he sat on a chair near the window and raised the bottle to his lips. His hands were shaking badly and he shivered despite the warming sensation in his abdomen from the liquor. He looked through the window to the street where Alma

83

and her husband would return and he tried not to think what might happen when they did.

Somewhere on the lower floor a clock struck one. He tipped the bottle up to his lips once more and discovered it was empty. Immediately he felt cold and lost —until he remembered the buffet in the dining room where an additional supply was kept.

He made the trip down the dark stairs and back again without difficulty. And as he drank from the new bottle — an entire quart—he felt the desire growing strongly again. He had to have Alma—he absolutely had to have her. Nothing else was important. She did things to him that no other woman could ever do and sometimes, even when he was tired, she made him more proud of himself than he had ever been before in his life.

He began to feel very good, very strong.

Rising from the chair he paced before the window, looking down at the dark wet street, wishing they would return now, this very minute when he felt so strong— strong enough to do whatever Alma demanded.

chapter 9

Even at one o'clock the party was still loud and boister-
ous, and everybody, including Norman, was having a
big time. The Dockstaders lived in a large Early Ameri-
can house and they'd rolled back the rugs in two rooms
for dancing. In the dining room there was dancing to
the Victrola, to such new hit songs as *Valencia* and
Fifty Million Frenchmen Can't Be Wrong. In the living
room a new radio, the first one Alma had ever seen with
a built-in speaker, supplied an unlimited number of fox
trots and an occasional turkey trot and waltz. The Dockstaders weren't stingy with their gin, rum, and beer and
they set up a buffet counter in the dining room where
the guests helped themselves to a post-midnight lunch of
knockwurst and potato salad.

Alma danced once with Norman and found it easy to
smile at him the rest of the evening and to carry on the
pretense that things were wonderful between them.
Several times, she let him finish her drink when the other
men invited her to dance. She kept a careful tabulation
and when she saw Norman down his seventh highball,

she knew everything was going to work out perfectly. Norman never got drunk, but he did grow exceptionally mellow and sleepy after half a dozen drinks. There would be no need to run the risk of giving him a sleeping powder after they got home, something which might not work anyway.

As for herself, she did not need liquor to add to her excitement. She spaced her drinks over the evening, finishing only two and sipping a little of the others. She danced at least once with every male present and enjoyed several extra turns around the floor with a good-looking young man who reminded her a lot of Bill Riddle, the first fellow she'd ever enjoyed making love with. By one-thirty, as the first couples were beginning to depart, her excitement was strong and vibrant.

"How about once more around?" asked the good-looking young man while the radio was playing, *In A Little Spanish Town.*

"Anything you say, hon," she replied.

And even though Norman might be watching, she leaned her head against the young man's shoulder and let him hold her tightly. It was so nice to be popular and in demand. And before long she would be able to do this as often as she liked, dance with as many young men as she wanted and spend all the money she wanted without worrying about explaining it to Norman.

She decided they should leave about quarter to two, neither too early nor too late. Enough couples remained to appreciate with chuckles and comments the pleasant domestic scene the Chryslers presented as they departed. Eileen, who had been put to bed with the Dockstader children, continued to sleep while Norman carried her over his shoulder past the couples who were still dancing. Alma held his other arm like a dutiful, devoted spouse and put her fur wrap over Eileen's legs as they went down the front steps into the rain.

During the drive home her excitement mounted so high it was extremely difficult to remain seated calmly on the cushion. She had not been so excited since that night when she was twenty-three and had her first party with Bill Riddle. She'd felt this same delicious wickedness that night and it had been raining, too, just as heavily, when she slipped out of the apartment after supper. That was when she and Norman were living on West Chestnut Street about four years after their marriage. It was the first time she'd ever made love to any one other than Norman, and it had been a great awakening. Until then she had never even suspected that making love could be so much fun. Norman, grooved in his dull routines, had been working nights at the magazine office, and not once, even then, did he inquire about how she spent some of her nights. It had been very easy to slip up the back steps to the apartment of Bill Riddle, whose folks were away every night running their delicatessen. Bill was only nineteen, very good-looking and very mature for his years. He had taught her to do things Norman could never have appreciated, even if she had given him the chance.

"Nice party, wasn't it," said Norman, filling the car with smoke from the Cuban cigar Mr. Dockstader had given him. He was so relaxed that for once he wasn't picking a fight with her on their way home, the way he usually did.

"Very nice," she said, but she didn't mean the party they'd just left. She was remembering those parties with Bill Riddle and the thrills she had, until the night she'd found the back door to his folks' apartment locked. She bit her lip, remembering how terrible she had felt when she found out later that he had another girl in there, Linda Haagensen, who was seventeen.

"You're too old for me, Alma," he'd told her the next day, laughing at her. "Gee whiz, you're almost five years older than me."

It had been one of the most upsetting, most insulting experiences of her life, but she'd fixed him. She'd written an anonymous letter to his folks, mailing it to the delicatessen, telling them what was going on every night at their apartment. That fixed good-looking, young Bill

87

Riddle right then and there. His folks had banished him to the farm of his grandparents in Maryland. How he must have hated it, soiling his tender hands as he shoveled manure, dipped sheep and labored like a slave in the sweet potato fields.

"What time is it?" Norman asked, as they turned onto their own street.

She looked at her watch. "Two. Exactly."

"Pretty damn late." Yawning, he failed, as usual, to put his hand over his mouth. "Got to get up early. Going fishing."

She almost felt like giggling at him. *Oh, no, you're not,* she thought, and the sensation of wickedness rose deliciously in the pit of her stomach.

She stared ahead through the windshield, looking up at the bedroom window of their house as they approached, although she knew it was much too dark and rainy to see Bud. But he was there, of that she was certain.

He *had* to be there.

chapter 10

Up in the bedroom, Ward stopped pacing as soon as the headlights turned in from the street and came along the driveway.

Without warning, terror leaped up within him and his desire to be strong and resolute melted quickly away. He began to shake. *What are you doing in this house?* a voice demanded, and his fear did not lessen when he realized it was his own voice. He leaped back from the window and fled toward the stairs. Halfway down, he remembered it was pouring rain and he couldn't go out minus his overcoat and hat. He ran back toward the bedroom, tripping in his frenzy on the top step, almost dropping the bottle. In the darkness of the closet he couldn't find his hat. Leaving without it, he threw his coat over his arm and started down the steps a second time.

Too late. Already there were footsteps at the side door and the sound of a key turning in the lock.

Back up the steps he fled, unable to breathe, choking on the air locked in his lungs. He ran to the bedroom and crouched on the floor in the darkest shadow behind the bed.

He heard a switch click and saw dim, reflected light in the hall. He heard heavy footsteps on the stairs, and decided they were Norman's. He heard Alma's footsteps, light and brisk, and then the sound of a child's voice, Eileen's, protesting as she was put to bed.

A toilet flushed and, in another minute, he heard the sound of heavy shoes, Norman's shoes, being dropped on the floor in the adjacent bedroom. He heard bedsprings and a mattress creak under someone's weight, undoubtedly Norman's, and then the house became silent again.

He waited to flee into the rain and darkness outside, but he could not move. He cowered beside the bed, breathing fitfully, his whole body trembling.

He heard Alma steal into the bedroom.

"Bud?" she said softly. "Are you here?"

He could not trust himself to whisper a reply. He gestured to her. Then he rose and went to her, putting his arms around her, feeling the intense warmth of her through the silken negligee. Alma shivered against him and he sensed her excitement and nervousness.

"Oh, Mommy," he said. "I've been—"

She placed her palm over his mouth. "Be quiet. He's finishing his cigar. We'll have to wait."

He watched her vanish into the dimness of the hall. Returning to the shadows beside the bed, he sat on the floor and drank from the bottle. He felt miserable.

Before long she came back with the whispered information that Eileen was sound asleep and Norman had put out his cigar.

"We'll still have to wait," she said. "We'll wait until he turns over and is sleeping on his good ear." She paused. "Now come here, you little devil."

Helping him to his feet, she kissed him hotly on the mouth. Then she rubbed her cheek against his and he could smell her perfume, its gardenia fragrance heightened by the warmth of her skin.

90

"Did you find the things?" she whispered. "Under the pillows?"

"Yes."

"The sash weight?"

"Yes."

"Did you bring the wire and the chloroform?"

"Yes."

"You've been drinking, haven't you?"

"Yes, I have, God damn it." His voice rose in intensity. "And if you think I'm—"

"Quiet, Bud!" Her hand, warmer than before, covered his mouth. "You *are* going through with it, aren't you?"

He did not reply.

"Well, aren't you?"

"Maybe."

"I'll say you are!" Her lips came closer to his ear. "You know what will happen if you don't! You'll never see me again at the hotel! You'll never see me again—ever!"

"I know, I know!" he said, miserably.

"And you want to, don't you?" He felt her hands moving at the front of her negligee, but he didn't realize she had unfastened it until she placed his hand upon her breast, pressing it hard into the uncovered flesh. *"Don't you?"*

Almost immediately he was reminded of Peony and that day long ago when she had pressed his hand against her breast in almost the same way. And he remembered his failure.

"Yes!" he said. "Yes, God damn it! Let's do it now! Let's have a party now!"

"No, you devil!" she giggled softly. "Later. After it's over, we'll get good and plastered and we'll have the best party ever! Now wait while I take another look at the Governor."

In less than a minute she returned.

"He's asleep." Her whisper was jubilant. "Sound asleep on his good ear. He won't hear a thing."

"What time is it?"

"Quarter to three."

"He can't be sound asleep yet. There hasn't been time enough."

"But he is, Bud. He is!"

"I don't care. I don't want to rush it. We'll wait fifteen more minutes." He raised the quart bottle and in the dim light from the hall saw that it was only a fourth full. "Do you want a drink?"

"No."

Sitting on the bed, he took a long pull and experienced a good reaction, felt his throat grow hot, felt the good heat of it in his belly.

"All right," she said reluctantly. "In fifteen minutes."

She sat sideways on the chair near the doorway, elbows resting on the wooden back, legs crossed, and in the dimness of the room she looked exactly like a silent figure on a photo negative.

He took another drink and it seemed to loosen his memory. He began to remember his failure, all his failures, those at school when he couldn't make the baseball team or even the track team because he was too small. He remembered the jibes and the insults of the bigger boys as they flaunted their muscles on the field. He felt his face flush as he remembered Peony again and was certain, as he'd always been, that she'd told the bigger boys about his failure up on the grassy slope behind the school. He could still hear her laughter—that damned girlish, ridiculous laughter. And there were those other failures, the lost jobs, the lost sales accounts. And there had been more laughter, men laughing behind his back when they turned down a sale, men making bad jokes about his size, implying that his virility was of similar proportions.

Rising to his feet, he took another drink and then he gazed across the room at Alma.

"It's time," she whispered. "Are you ready?"

He knew the fifteen minutes hadn't passed, but suddenly he didn't care.

He nodded.

She came to his side. She was breathing quickly, through her mouth, the way she did sometimes when they made love. In her eyes the light from the hall was reflected with a strange brilliance, a deep glow that was animal-like in intensity. It reminded him of a leopard he'd once seen in a zoo.

"Here," she commanded, "put these on."

She handed him the cotton gloves that had been on the bed. Her fingers, as they touched his, were extremely warm.

He put the gloves on.

"Have you got it?" she whispered.

"Got what?"

"The sash weight, you fool!"

He picked it up and was astonished at how heavy it was.

"Yes."

"All right. I'll bring the other things."

He watched her put a stick of gum into her mouth and begin to chew it nervously. Then she removed the cap from the chloroform and picked up the other objects— the cotton waste, the coil of wire and a pair of pliers which he hadn't realized were on the bed.

"All right." He heard her draw in her breath sharply. "Now!"

He held the sash weight with both hands and felt her hand grasp his elbow, guiding him into the hallway. He did not feel excited. He did not feel anything, other than the fact that he was a little drunker than usual, and that his legs were relaxed and loose.

The door to the master bedroom was closed but not latched.

Alma pushed with her elbow and it opened on hinges which functioned silently.

Grasping his arm again, she guided him inside and he saw that it was a large bedroom, better lighted than the other one because the light from the hall shone in more directly. His eyes made out the high bed, its scrollwork footboard and a shadowy mound beneath the blankets.

Ward's heart gave a great lurch as he realized what the mound was. It was the first time he had ever seen Norman and he was astonished at how large a man he was, how thick he was through the shoulders.

He felt Alma pushing him toward the bed, guiding him toward the headboard. Because of a flap of dark blanket, he could not make out Norman's features, but it was apparent that Norman was lying sideways, his head only partly on the pillow.

"Now!" whispered Alma and there was a tremendous urgency in her voice.

As he raised the sash weight, grasping it tightly with both hands, the blood thrashed at his temples, making his ears ring with pressure, forcing him to open his mouth and draw in air. But the weight felt good in his hands, its very heaviness giving him strength, and he raised it higher and stepped closer to the bed.

And now he saw how really big Norman was and he was glad Norman was big, especially because he was as big as the biggest athletes at school had been, as powerful as the most powerful of his tormentors had been.

But he was not afraid now.

He was not afraid of Norman or any of the others.

He raised the sash weight high in the air.

He brought the weight crashing down toward the sleeping head and it was so heavy it started to slip from his fingers.

It struck the side of Norman's head.

It struck bone and then glanced off.

A roar came from the bedclothes, the bellow of a man in terrible pain.

With horror Ward realized that the blow had almost missed! At best, it had merely stunned Norman.

Norman's head twisted wildly from side to side, and Alma screamed.

"Hit him! Hit him again!"

Ward tried to retrieve the sash weight, but his fingers

became frantically tangled in the blanket and he could not find it.

Norman looked about him with crazed eyes, trying to sit up. And Ward knew that Norman mustn't be allowed to sit up, because if he did it would mean failure, complete failure added to all those other failures.

Ward threw himself on the bed. He straddled Norman's twisting body and somehow his fingers found the thick, muscular throat. With all his strength he squeezed, but it was not enough, not nearly enough, and he felt Norman's hands striking him, smashing at him, trying to dislodge him. And then he felt something drawing tight about his own throat, crushing his own windpipe. Paralyzed with terror, he suddenly realized that Norman had seized his necktie and was strangling him with it.

"Mommy, Mommy!" he cried. "For God's sakes, Mommy, help me!"

He saw Alma pick up the sash weight. He felt the necktie being drawn tighter around his throat, felt the big, rough hands drawing his face closer to Norman's. From the edge of his eye, he saw Alma raise the weight and smash it across her husband's forehead.

Norman's head was driven deep into the pillow, but the blow was not enough. Shaking, the eyes almost swelling from their sockets, the head rose powerfully once more from the pillow and the big hands pulled harder on Ward's necktie.

"Bastard!" Alma screamed. "Heinie bastard!"

Again she raised the weight. And before it descended, Norman's eyes recognized her and were blurred with anguish and bewilderment at what his wife was doing to him.

"Jesus!" he said. "My God, Alma! Alma—"

The sash weight struck with such force that Ward, whose face was inches from Norman's, could feel the contact of metal against bone. Tight around Norman's throat, his fingers felt Norman's neck muscles bulge and contract with reaction to each blow. It was unbelieveable that she could do it so many times—raise the huge weight again and again and bring it down with such crushing force.

It went on and on—a black dream of agony.

Ward did not know how much time passed before he found himself standing beside the bed, shoulders slumped, staring at the figure tangled in the sheet, smelling something sharply sweet that hurt his nostrils.

Norman was no longer moving. Ward felt Alma's presence beside him, heard her breathing rapidly, panting like an animal in heat.

He stared at the figure on the bed, saw that Norman was lying on his stomach, his hands tied behind his back with a towel. The face, dark with blood, was partially turned and he saw the cotton waste stuffed into both nostrils and realised what he smelled was the sweet chloroform that had been poured upon the cotton.

He stared at Alma and saw that the front of her negligee was streaked with blood from the shoulders to below her knees. He stared at himself and saw that his shirt and tie were spattered with dark red. His hands felt wet and he discovered that the cheap cloth gloves were soaked with blood.

"Oh, my God!" he said.

"Help me!" Alma cried. "Help me tie him up!"

But he could not help her. He watched her go to the closet, find one of Norman's neckties and knot it around Norman's unmoving ankles.

He felt very weak and sick. Stumbling into the bathroom, he threw up into the toilet and then leaned against the wall, moaning and clutching his stomach with both hands.

The bathroom door opened and Alma came in. In the bright light from the overhead bulb, her eyes were glazed and dull-looking.

"Look at that." She pointed weakly to his shirt. "Look at all that blood."

She gazed at herself, discovered the red stains on her negligee.

"Oh, my God!" she wailed. "What are we going to do? Look at me! Look at your shirt!"

He could not reply. He leaned against the wall near the toilet, shaking his head, trying to think but completely muddled.

"Take it off!" Alma said. "I'll get you one of his."

Following her back to the bedroom, he removed his necktie and shirt and dropped them on the floor. She took a blue shirt from a bureau drawer and he put it on, his trembling fingers moving awkwardly on the buttons, his shoulders feeling small and puny in the folds of the shirt which was many sizes too large. Numbly he watched her shed the negligee, place it on top of his shirt and then don a horrible blood-red Chinese robe with a dragon coiling across the front.

For many minutes they scrubbed their hands in the washbowl.

And then they went downstairs.

They did not speak.

A milk wagon rolled by on the wet street outside, its metal wheels splashing through a puddle, the horse's hoofs making a crisp clop-clop sound on the paving. Ward wanted to lean back against the sofa but he could not. He sat up stiffly, his mind sobering, gradually allowing itself to dwell on what had happened upstairs. He could not shield his mind from the facts. It knew clearly now, horribly and thoroughly, what had happened upstairs. A quotation of his mother's began to uncoil from a cove deep within his brain, finally coming into full awareness. It was not the familiar quotation: *Thou Shalt Not Kill.* It was another, one he hadn't thought about for years: *Ye shall keep the Sabbath; every one that profaneth it shall surely be put to death.* And this day was now the Sabbath. This dark, black day was the Sabbath and the terrible thing upstairs had occurred on the Sabbath.

He spoke it aloud. "Ye shall keep the Sabbath."

"What?" Alma turned and looked at him, her jaws

working slowly on the chewing gum. "What did you say?"

He repeated it.

"Oh, shut up," she said. "Shut up and think about what we have to do."

For another two minutes, they were silent.

"We've got to go back up there," she said. "We've got to make it look like burglary. Did you bring that newspaper, the Italian one?"

He nodded.

"Come on," she said. "You've got to come with me."

He followed her up the stairs. At the doorway to the bedroom they paused, staring fearfully at the heavy-shouldered form tangled in the sheet and blankets.

"My God," said Alma suddenly. "What if he's not dead?"

Ward said nothing. He began to shiver.

"He's got to be," she said. "This has got to go through or I'm ruined."

chapter 11

After Bud left, Alma forced herself to wait for a full half-hour. She lay on the bed in her mother's room, legs tied with two of Norman's neckties, her hands bound behind her back with strips of cheesecloth. Another strip of the cheesecloth, tasting very much like straw, was fastened across her mouth and knotted at her neck.

Silently, her tongue making the cloth damp, she cursed Bud for being so helpless, for not drawing the knots tighter.

It was the longest half hour of her life, but she had to give him enough time to catch his bus. She owed him that much, even though he'd done such a miserable job. The bedroom was cold from the rain which continued outside and she shivered and trembled and tried to fix accurately in her mind what she would say and do when the time came.

Finally there was enough ugly gray morning light in the room for her to read the small alarm clock on the shelf beside the bed.

Seven-thirty. It was time.

As she lowered herself to the floor and wriggled toward the hallway, she did not have to feign excitement. Her whole body quivered with anticipation and she thumped her feet excitedly against the throw rug in the hall, welcoming the noise she made because it meant the strain and suspense would soon be over.

She began to shout.

"Help, help!" Her words were muffled by the cheesecloth. "Eileen, help me!"

Waking her daughter was more difficult than she expected. Tired from the long party of the night before, the little girl did not stir until Alma wriggled to the door of her bedroom and struck the wooden panel again and again with her bound feet.

The door opened a crack and Eileen's blue eyes peered out, half-asleep. Instantly, they widened.

"Mama!" she cried.

"Burglars!" Alma screamed through the cheesecloth. "Help me, Eileen!"

After that, the events went off more or less as expected. Terrified, weeping almost hysterically, Eileen slipped the cloth gag from her mother's mouth. Then she did as Alma commanded her—running to their neighbors next door, the Ernstbruners.

Within a few minutes the Chrysler house was transformed from gray Sunday morning silence into bedlam. Wearing a bathrobe and heavy, unlaced boots, Mr. Ernstbruner, who was an exceedingly fat meat-market owner, shook the whole staircase as he hurried, puffing, to give Alma assistance. His wife remained downstairs, supposedly to comfort Eileen, who was still weeping uncontrollably. But Mrs. Ernstbruner, shrilling questions to her husband in German, demanding to know what had happened, was a comfort to no one.

"A burglar!" gasped Alma as Mr. Ernstbruner untied her legs and hands. "Help Norman! I think something terrible has happened to him!"

She remained seated on the hall floor as Mr. Ernstbruner hurried to the master bedroom.

One glance through the doorway was sufficient for Mr. Ernstbruner. In near panic, he bolted back down the hall, his fat cheeks pale and shaking, wanting to know where the telephone was so he could notify the police.

"And call a doctor!" moaned Alma. "There's a terrible pain in my head!"

The doctor arrived first, a pleasant young man who lived in the neighborhood and who smelled nicely of medicines and chemicals. He spent less than a minute in the master bedroom. When he came out into the hall, shaking his head in that somber way doctors use when the news is bad, Alma was so relieved she had little difficulty loosing her emotions and carrying on like a bereft wife.

When the police came, the young doctor was still ministering to her, giving her pills to quiet her nerves and applying a cloth dipped in cold water to her forehead.

The two officers were also young. They were tall and very good-looking in their blue uniforms. They were very sympathetic and suggested that Alma rest downstairs on the sofa while they completed their investigation in the bedroom.

When they came down to the living room afterward, Alma couldn't help noticing their appreciative glances. The Chinese robe did fit her very well, the thin cloth being sufficiently tight across the bosom, and her bare legs were attractively displayed against the soft pillows.

She repeated her story for the officers, keeping it simple so the facts wouldn't be contradictory or confusing. Averting her eyes, she kept her voice low and husky.

"I—I don't really know what it was that woke me," she said. "A noise, some kind of a noise. I thought it might be Eileen. I thought she might be sick from something she ate at the party. So I got up and started down the hall. And—" she touched her handkerchief to the corners of her eyes. "And then I saw this shadow. That's all I saw of him—a shadow, and it was awful—" She shuddered. "He hit me. He dragged me into Mother's room and threw me on the bed. He hit me again and I must have passed out because I don't remember any more. Nothing. I just can't—"

Pressing her face against the sofa's cushioned back, she wept for part of a minute. She did not overdo it. She wept quietly, like Carole Lombard did in that movie with Edmund Lowe, and was rewarded with comments of sympathy from the young officers as well as Mr. and Mrs. Ernstbruner.

"It must have been the same man I saw!" declared Mrs. Ernstbruner shrilly. "I saw him last Monday night, hanging around in the alley. He was a big man, wasn't he, Mrs. Chrysler, big and tall and slouchy-looking?"

Alma nodded. "I think so. I didn't get too good a look at him. I think he might have been an Italian."

"Thank you very much, Mrs. Chrysler," said one of the young officers. "It certainly looks like the work of the same burglar we've had reports on before."

Continuing to weep quietly, brushing at the tears with her fingertips, Alma found it easy to conceal the warm glow of triumph within her. It hadn't been nearly as simple as she'd imagined it would be. But with the police convinced, the worst of it was definitely over. She leaned back against the cushions, crossed her legs and modestly smoothed the hem of her robe down across her knee. None of her movements were missed by the eyes of the young officers and she knew exactly what they would say to one another when they got outside. *Some dish, ain't she? And did you get a good look at them gams? Man, oh, man!*

The two officers closed their notebooks and went to the front door.

But they did not leave.

Instead they admitted several more officers in uniforms and a number who were, she supposed, plainclothes men. She was quite certain they would finish their work and leave shortly, but instead she heard the sound of more

102

automobiles arriving outside and soon half a dozen more men came in and began moving through the house.

Rising from the sofa, she excused herself politely as she passed in front of Mrs. Ernstbruner and went to the window.

She was astonished at the amount of activity outside. Over a dozen police cars were parked in the street and it looked like the whole neighborhood—gangs of children, plus men and women in church finery and Sunday sport togs—thronged the sidewalk in front of the house. A vast number of police uniforms milled about, trampling Norman's prized Warner rosebushes and crushing the bed of green daffodil shoots. She felt a small dart of panic that so many officers had been called out for what was obviously a simple case of burglary, but she was certain there would be no difficulty so long as she kept her facts in order.

By ten o'clock there were as many officers inside as outside and she had repeated her story nearly a dozen times. A surprising number of newspaper reporters and photographers were present, asking endless questions, taking endless pictures.

Two doctors from the Police Department examined her head, asked kind, sympathic questions and then consulted with the young neighborhood doctor who still hadn't departed.

"Now, Mrs. Chrysler, shall we go over it once more?" asked the dumpy, badly-dressed man who had been introduced as Mr. Tomiskey, from the D. A.'s office. She noticed that the other officers regarded him quite highly despite his shabby appearance.

She repeated the facts, keeping them in the same order as before.

"We must have a better description of the man," said Tomiskey. "Can't you describe his nose or his hair?"

She shook her head. "No, sir, I'm sorry. He was rough-looking, that's all I know. He might have been an Italian."

"With a mustache?"

"Yes, I think he had a mustache."

She decided she definitely didn't like Tomiskey's eyes. He was an older man, fifty-five or sixty at least, and his caramel-brown eyes were never at rest. He was gentle, however, and extremely courteous.

"Shall we go upstairs, Mrs. Chrysler?" he asked. "I'd like you to show us exactly how you were tied up and how you managed to crawl down the hall.

She did exactly as requested, complied with every request, answered every question and controlled her temper even though she saw that Tomiskey was altering his inquiries slightly, trying to force her to change her replies.

After that they took her into her mother's bedroom and let her sit in the rocking chair near the bed. They brought her coffee, granted her wish for a stick of clove chewing gum, but they did not permit her to leave the bedroom except for a brief trip to the bathroom. They let her mother visit her for a few minutes, but it was a terrible scene, with Mrs. Jansson carrying on hysterically, embracing her, giving her no help whatsoever.

The questioning went on and on, throughout the morning and into the afternoon, and she found it increasingly difficult to understand why it was taking so long and why so many officers, almost dozens of them, were prowling the house. From the tone of Tomiskey's questions, she knew she was in serious, even critical, trouble, but she did not allow herself to be frightened into changing her story. Several times Tomiskey stepped out into the hall and she heard his low-voiced conversation with some of the other officers.

After one of his trips into the hall, Tomiskey returned with another officer whom he introduced as Detective Yost.

"We found a strange object in the cellar," said Tomiskey. "It was in a toolbox and covered with ashes." He paused. "A sash weight. Do you have any idea how it got there?"

"No, I don't." She kept her voice cool and unemotional.

"It's spotted with dried blood," added Detective Yost. "How do you account for that?".

"I don't know anything about it," she said calmly, but she felt a tremendous pressure in the room as though something were closing in on her."

"You claim the burglar knocked you unconscious," said Tomiskey, "but none of the doctors found a scratch on you. Isn't that rather strange?"

"It doesn't look at all like burglary," said Detective Yost.

"Why not?" Alma realized her voice was snappish, but she definitely didn't like the detective's attitude or his manner.

"We see lots of burglaries." Detective Yost shrugged. "They are not done this way. The doors were not forced. Your husband was attacked in a number of different ways, when one would have been quite enough. And I can't for the life of me understand why that pistol was left on the bed beside him."

"What was so strange about that?" From the glance that passed between the two officers she knew she shouldn't have asked the question, but now that she was committed she glared at them boldly, and demanded that they answer.

"It's quite simple." Detective Yost shrugged once more. "The gun has your husband's fingerprints on it, making it look like he tried to defend himelf with it. But, believe me, Mrs. Chrysler, no burglar would leave a weapon lying beside his victim, running the risk of the victim coming to and picking it up. Entirely too risky."

Suddenly she felt nauseous and weak, and she decided she hated these two men more than anyone in her life. Almost as much as she hated Norman. She tried to sit back in the rocking chair, tried to look calm, but there was so much perspiration on her palms she found it difficult to grasp the arm rests.

"Here's something else that puzzles me." Opening his handkerchief, Detective Yost displayed a jeweled stickpin. "How do you account for this being found on the floor of the bedroom, Mrs. Chrysler?"

"It's my husband's," she said.

"Oh?" The detective looked doubtful. "But the initial is W."

She hesitated only long enough to take a deep breath. And then it was wonderful the way her mind came agilely to her rescue, supplying a perfect answer.

"That's the initial of Winnie," she replied. "She was Norman's fiancée, but she died. He wore it in her memory."

"I see," said Detective Yost, but he did not appear to be convinced.

"And here's something else that turned up," said Tomiskey. "We found this address book in one of the bureau drawers. Is this your handwriting, Mrs. Chrysler?"

She glanced at the small book. "Yes."

"And these names," he continued. "Who are all these men? Ralph Shrank, Scotty McNally, Robert Crenshaw, James Van Der Most, Ward Green, George Cline and all the rest. Who are they?"

"Acquaintances of mine."

"You mean you're acquainted with all these men?" Tomiskey appeared to be impressed. "Why, madame, there's over two dozen names here."

"I've known some of them for years," she said. "They're just friends."

"Who's Ralph Shrank?"

"A building contractor."

"Who's Scotty McNally?"

"Another building contractor."

"Robert Crenshaw?"

"I haven't seen him for years."

"Ward Green?"

"A salesman."

"What kind of a salesman?"

"Corsets."

"Who is James Van Der Most?"

"A clerk."

106

Tomiskey read through the entire list, asking the same questions about each name. And then he read through the list a second and a third time.

Afterward he paused and his brown eyes, never at rest, studied her carefully.

"Mrs. Chrysler," he said. "Did you realize that each time I read a particular one of these names you looked down at the floor? And when you answered my questions about him your voice definitely trembled, were you aware of that?"

"I don't believe I did."

"Yes, Mrs. Chrysler, you did. Would you like to know which name it was?"

"Not particularly."

"I think I should tell you, Mrs. Chrysler. It was Ward Green. And are you aware, Mrs. Chrysler, that Ward Green's initial is W.—the same as on the stickpin?"

For a half dozen heartbeats, the room was silent. From the hall came the low hum of the voices of many other officers, and Alma was visibly startled when an abrupt rap sounded on the door.

Tomiskey opened it and stepped outside. She heard him begin an urgent whispered conversation with another officer, their voices too low to be understood.

In a moment he returned. He shut the door gently, then turned and faced her.

"Mrs. Chrysler," he began. He folded his arms across the badly-wrinkled serge lapels of his suit. "It is my duty to inform you that Mr. Ward Green has been arrested."

She felt stifled, as though a hand were crushing her throat, and it was impossible to remain calmly in the rocking chair. She half-rose, then sat back down.

"And Mr. Green has confessed," said Tomiskey quietly. "He has confessed everything. He has informed us that *you*, Mrs. Chrysler, helped him murder your husband."

For an instant, she felt no reaction. No reaction whatsoever.

Then came rage, violent rage, which made her spring from the chair. She fell upon Tomiskey, pummeling him

107

with her fists, driving him backwards until his shoulders struck the door.

"Lies!" she screamed. "He lied! *He* killed Norman! *He* did it! And he said he would kill me if I told! I tried to stop him, but he was like a madman! *He* killed Norman! *He* killed my husband! I tried to stop him! I tried but—"

She stopped. She backed away from Tomiskey. She realized that in her anger she might have said too much.

"Thank you," said Tomiskey. "Thank you very much, Mrs. Chrysler."

chapter 12

When he left the train at Syracuse, Ward Green went directly to his room at the hotel. He was so exhausted, his calves and thighs ached as if he had walked the entire distance. He needed a drink, needed it so badly his throat felt swollen, but he did not take one. He had not had a drink during the train ride either; it was punishment for the events of the terrible night.

He sat alone in the dimness of the hotel room, the lights extinguished. The weight upon his mind was enormous, a vast mass which threatened to plunge through the very tissues of his brain. He still could not believe it. Perhaps it had not happened; perhaps it had happened to someone else, another man, and he merely thought it had happened to himself. But through the tangled thoughts came the sound of his mother's voice, rising and falling: *"Ye shall keep the Sabbath."*

And this was still the Sabbath. And he did not need to look at his hands to see the dark red stains in the crevices around his fingernails. The dark red stains which no amount of scrubbing on the train had been able to remove. And through his mind ran other words, a stream of them: *"Father, may we be ever mindful that it is in loving our fellow man that we truly love Thee . . ."* He had always loved his fellow man; he still loved his fellow man. But if he did, how possibly could he explain the terrible, terrible events of this Sabbath?

He could no longer stand the terrible dryness of his throat. From his coat, which he had dropped on the floor, he removed the bottle of whiskey Alma had given him to drink on the train. It was a pint, still full. He took a long drink, then another, but it tasted sweetish and he decided Alma's bootleg druggist had sold her part of a bad batch.

Suddenly he could no longer stand the dim silence of the hotel room's walls. He needed company; somebody to talk to; somebody to keep his mind off things. He walked down the corridor and rapped on the door to 377, Ed Potter's room.

"Ed," he said, "can I come in a minute?"

"Sure," came Ed's voice. "It's unlocked."

He found Ed lying on the bed, reading the Sunday papers, his sample case open on the nightstand, pink sales slip carbons spread around it.

"Mister, you look punk," Ed said. "That must've been some hot date you had." Ward nodded.

"I fixed it up for you," Ed said. "I phoned your missus and told her you'd been called to Albany for a sales meeting."

"Thanks, Ed. You got a drink handy?"

"Sure. In my case."

It was a bottle of gin, not much better quality than Alma's pint. He didn't drink much of it because he was discovering that liquor wasn't what he wanted. He didn't know what he wanted. Despite his exhaustion, he didn't want to rest, or even sit down. It had been a long time since his last meal, but he didn't want to eat. Nor did he feel like talking to Ed, now that he was here.

Finally he let Ed persuade him to go down to the hotel

dining room for dinner, but he couldn't eat the boiled potatoes and roast lamb which the waitress brought.

"You look sick," Ed said. "I've never seen you look so bad. What in blazes did you do in Albany—go to bed with three blondes?"

Ed grinned and tried to make Ward do the same, but Ward merely shook his head.

"I didn't go to Albany," he said.

"Then where did you go?"

Ward did not reply.

He was such poor company that Ed left him shortly after dinner and returned to his room.

Ward sat in an upholstered chair in the lobby. For an interval which had no beginning and no end, he stared at the yellow illuminated face of a large wall clock on the far side of the room. He was aware that the clock had Roman numerals, but not once during the evening was he fully aware of what time it was. He wondered if he should take the money Alma had given him, the seventy dollars from her husband's wallet, and buy another train ticket, perhaps one to Ohio or Kansas or even Colorado.

But he did not move from the chair.

Much later he noticed that the clock's hands pointed to twelve. He went wearily to his room and began to undress and when he heard the knuckles tap his door he thought it was probably Ed Potter.

It was not Ed Potter. It was three men with grim, intense faces who announced that they were police officers.

"We're taking you to the station," they said.

He was not at all surprised to see them; actually, he had expected them to arrive much sooner.

There was no conversation during the ride in the black Hupmobile to the Syracuse Police Station. But once he was in the interrogation room, an airless chamber that reeked of bad plumbing, there was no end to the talk, no end to the questions which went on for hours. They demanded to know the intimate details of his relationship

111

with Alma. Their minds were filthy with questions. They insisted on knowing how many times he and Alma had met in hotel rooms and what they had done there. They demanded to know why he had helped her kill her husband.

"Gentlemen," he replied, "this is ridiculous. I haven't been near her house for months."

"We know you were there," one of the officers insisted. "We've got the stub of the Pullman ticket you came back on. Now why don't you come clean with us?"

They could not understand how he could be so calm. That was because there was no way for them to know that the events of the night before had wrung the last drippings of emotion from him.

He told them nothing. He lied, but not for himself. He lied for Alma. It was the very least he could do. In a situation like this it was necessary for the man to be strong. It was necessary for the man to protect the woman.

It was nearly dawn when the officers gave up on him and put him in a cell. The cell was more comfortable than the interrogation room had been, largely because the plumbing did not smell as bad.

He did not sleep.

At nine o'clock in the morning they allowed him to have a visitor.

It was Ed Potter who came up to the door of the cell, his face pale and shaken.

"My God, Ward!" Ed said. "Have you seen the papers this morning? Nothing but headlines and more headlines! All about you and that woman!"

Ward stared at him blankly.

"Did you?" Ed's voice lowered to a rough whisper. "Did you do what they say, Ward?"

Ward closed his eyes slowly, then opened them.

"Yes, Ed. I think I did it."

"My God, Ward!" Ed reached through the bars and touched his friend's hand. "Ward, why did you do it?"

"I don't know."

112

There was nothing more for them to say after that. And soon Ed departed, after promising to do all he could to help.

Half an hour later the officers took Ward down the front steps of the Police Station, to the black Hupmobile at the curb. There was a crowd on the steps and sidewalk, people with strangely curious expressions on their faces. It wasn't until he was on the back seat, an officer on either side of him, that he realized the crowd had gathered to look at him.

"That's him," he heard one of the voices say. "That's Ward Green."

chapter 13

Never in her life had Alma Chrysler known such excitement. The excitement began each morning at six, sometimes earlier, when the matrons awakened her. There was never any way of knowing what each day would bring—visits from attorneys, officials of the jail, famous writers, photographers, even ministers.

At first, when she had been a nobody, just another prisoner, she had been very sad, suffering from the blues all day, regretting her foolishness in falling for Tomiskey's trick. It had been a very miserable trick, the way he'd told her that Ward Green had been arrested and that he'd confessed, making her so angry that she said things she shouldn't have. Tomiskey had lied. Ward hadn't been arrested until much, much later and he hadn't told the police anything for hours and hours.

But now, of course, everything was so different. Now she was a celebrity. Now she had a cell of her own, a very comfortable one with good light, where she could pore over her newspapers and magazines as long as she wished. It was really remarkable how much differently the matrons treated her now, letting her visit with her mother every day, bringing her coffee almost whenever she wished, bringing her chewing gum, bringing her the gifts from her admirers.

And she had many, many admirers—men knew she was an unfortunate woman, a woman terribly wronged by her lover and terribly tricked by the police. The gifts were very nice—flowers, candy, black lingerie, and many of the packages contained notes from perfect strangers, very affectionate, some with proposals of marriage. She had more gifts than she could possibly use, and the matrons loved her for the packages she turned over to them. Even the matrons knew how wronged she had been, how badly she had been treated by the police. The matrons were experts in these matters and as the days went by they became more and more certain that she would get off.

"They'll never convict you, honey," said Mrs. O'Rourke every morning when she came with the papers. "Everybody knows that terrible Ward Green did it. And, besides, honey, you're too pretty to be convicted. You're a mighty pretty gal, honey."

And that's what made it so exciting. Her attorneys, young Mr. Whitcomb and old Mr. Strawn, were positive, too. "Everything's on your side, Alma," Mr. Whitcomb told her. "Ward Green's confession will win it for us. And thank God for all this publicity. Do you realize, Alma, that your name is in the papers these days more often that President Coolidge's?"

Oh, she knew it, all right. At first, right after her arrest, the headlines had frightened her with their blackness, their exclamation points. She couldn't understand it then, any of it. She couldn't understand how one day she was just a housewife, just another mother of a nine-year-old girl, living like other women. And the next day she was famous, with mobs thronging to get a glimpse of her, with reporters pressing in to catch her every word and write it down, and photographers, her every expression.

When the trial started, her picture was in all the papers every day. Even in the papers in Chicago and in Miami and way out in San Francisco. And now it was no longer so difficult to understand. People were extremely interested in her. They were interested because she was pretty, because the trial promised to have plenty of sexy testimony, and because the reporters said she was fighting for her life. The reporters loved her, all right. They winked at her and openly admired her figure. They were very brash, some of them. "Look at those hips," she heard one say loudly right in the courtroom. "Je-sus! No wonder Ward Green had the hots for her!"

On the morning of the eleventh day of the trial, she awoke in her cell long before six, chilled with excitement. Because this was it—this was the day she was to take the stand and testify in her own behalf. She was so nervous she was unable to eat her breakfast and she didn't drink more than half a cup of coffee. She'd been drinking too much coffee lately and her nerves were suffering because of it, twitching in the night sometimes and making her perspire even in the mornings when it was cool.

She was cross when Mrs. O'Rourke finally arrived with the papers. Mrs. O'Rourke apologized for being late, explaining that she'd run into two female reporters in the jail corridor who'd badgered her for details about how her famed prisoner brushed her teeth and asked how she obtained bleach for her hair.

"I didn't tell them," said Mrs. O'Rourke. "I might have got into trouble."

"Thank you," said Alma crisply, pulling the papers from the matron's hand. "Thank you very much!"

The papers were full of predictions about what she would testify. The eleventh chapter of her biography, "By Alma Chrysler," was in the morning *Press-Bulletin*. *The New York Union-Telegram* printed another article by Fannie Hurst and there was comment by David

Belasco in the *Daily Express*. Mr. Belasco's words were very kind, calling her a poor, unfortunate woman—"drawn into this mess as she embarked on what she thought was to be the great romance of her life!" And, of course, there were the usual insults in some of the papers, calling her the blond sinner, the marble woman, the tiger woman. The *News-Press* had a new phrase this morning, a terrible one, calling her the bloody blonde. She promptly tore the copy to shreds and vowed not to read the *News-Press* any more.

Both Mr. Whitcomb and Mr. Strawn arrived early at the jail and they spent another hour going slowly over the questions and answers. "Excellent," said Mr. Whitcomb when they finished. "You'll do fine, Alma."

She spent the time from eight-thirty to nine on her nails and hair, changing from the drab jail frock into a dress which Mr. Whitcomb had chosen for her. It was entirely black, severely fashioned, with a high neck. Around her throat she wore a black rosary from which dangled a crucifix. She used just a touch of lipstick and no rouge or powder, leaving her face pale and becomingly sallow.

Outside the courthouse, the street and sidewalk were alive with people waiting to see her arrive. The officers had to drive the people back as she was taken to the entrance. Some of the more excited ones darted in between the officers, pleading for her autograph, and all around her there was a murmuring, a humming of voices and occasionally an insult shouted by some idiot on the fringes of the crowd.

"Gangway!" cried the uniformed lieutenant who directed her escort of officers. "Let Mrs. Chrysler through! Let Mrs. Chrysler through!"

In the corridor directly outside the courtroom, the crowd was more disgusting. People had been lined up since dawn waiting for seats inside, some paying as much as ten and twenty dollars to be among the first in line. But the most sickening by far were those who wore stickpins in their lapels, those dreadful miniature sash weights that were sold on every corner around the courthouse for ten cents each.

When she arrived at the counsel table, Ward was already there, sitting in the same chair that he occupied every day, less than a dozen feet from her own chair. His cheeks were very pallid, there were circles under his eyes and as usual his fingers held a black prayer book.

She did not speak to him. She had not spoken to him since the trial began and she did not intend to speak to him.

She gave him a single glance, the one that Mr. Whitcomb approved, a glance of hatred for the man who had killed her husband, but with a touch of pity for him so the people in the courtroom could see that her feelings were only human. He did not raise his eyes to look at her as she sat down.

She had expected to testify almost at once, steeling herself mentally for the ordeal. But much of the morning session was devoted to legal procedures and a long suspenseful statement by Mr. Whitcomb, who spoke in a low, intelligent voice, giving the jury the background of the Chryslers' unhappy, quarrelsome home life, telling why he and his legal colleagues had decided she must take the stand to explain how she was dragged into the crime. A noticeable murmur swept the jammed courtroom when Mr. Whitcomb added that he and his assistants would not deny that an adulterous relationship existed between Mrs. Chrysler and Ward Green, and that they would prove Ward Green had used that relationship for his own selfish, damnable purposes.

A much greater murmur, a wave of excited comment and whispers, rolled through the courtroom when the bailiff at last called her to take her place in the witness chair.

She walked very slowly. When she seated herself, she was careful to keep the skirt of her black silk dress from revealing more than the lower part of her calves. She looked once at the judge and once at the jury box and

118

then she kept her eyes averted, her fingers touching the rosary beads once and then coming to rest, clasped, in her lap.

It was not nearly as trying as she had expected. Mr. Whitcomb smiled at her, giving her confidence, and his questions were easy, exactly the same as those they had gone over during their meetings in the jail conference room. During the preliminary questions, the crowd was restless, but as soon as the name of Ward Green was mentioned the courtroom became silent with expectation.

"Now, Mrs. Chrysler," said Mr. Whitcomb, "you were unfaithful to your marriage vows with Ward Green, were you not?"

"Yes."

"Was he the only man who ever knew you carnally or knew you in that manner?"

"Yes."

At once a loud hum spread through the room and there was a shout from somewhere in the back which she couldn't understand.

"Excepting your husband?" continued Mr. Whitcomb.

"My husband," she said.

"Where was it that you first met Ward Green?"

"In Truzzillini's restaurant on Thirty-sixth Street."

"When was it that you met him there?"

"About two years ago."

"Who introduced you?"

"A gentleman by the name of Ralph Shrank."

"After that when was it that you met him again?"

"I should say it was two months later, possibly in August or September of that year."

"Do you recall the conversation you had with him the first time?"

"It was principally on getting a garment from his concern."

"What type of garment?"

"A corselet."

"And when did you become intimate with Mr. Green?"

119

"The third time we met. In September, at the Hotel Raleigh."

"And did you have other visits to hotels with him?"

"Yes."

The crowd became so noisy the bailiff called for order. From the rear of he room, a woman's voice shouted, "Shame! Shame!" but Alma did not let it upset her because Mr. Whitcomb had warned her that such outbursts might occur.

"Did Ward Green ever speak to you about leaving your husband and marrying him instead?"

"No."

"Did he ever say anything about getting rid of your husband?"

"Yes."

"When was the first time he said that?"

"In the early months of this year."

"And what did he say to you?"

"Well, he said lots to me. Once he sent me some poison and told me to give it to my husband. And many times he talked about how much insurance my husband had and how he would like to have some of that money. Of course, I never believed he meant anything by it then."

"You lent him money occasionally?"

"Yes."

"And he kept wanting more?"

"Yes, he said he wanted much more, that he needed a lot more. And he said if I didn't let him do what he wanted to do to my husband he would do something far worse."

"What did he mean?"

"He said he would kill me—and himself, too."

"Did you think he meant it?"

"Yes, I began to see that he might be serious. He had threatened before—last summer—to do the same thing."

Nodding thoughtfully, Mr. Whitcomb went to the counsel table, consulted some papers and then returned. His face, handsomely framed with prematurely gray hair at the temples, was very calm and again he smiled at her. She sat back in the chair and let herself relax slightly.

"Now, Mrs. Chrysler," he said, "would you describe the package Mr. Green gave you one day at the restaurant?"

"Yes. It was about two feet long and very heavy."

"And what was in that package?"

"A letter and a sash weight."

"And what did he say in the letter?"

"He said, 'I am coming over Friday night.' I do not recall exactly whether he said 'to do the job' or 'finish the Governor.' I cannot just recall, because those sayings had been said in so many of his letters."

"Were there any powders in that letter?"

"Yes, there were. He said I should give my husband one of those powders just before bedtime."

"And what did you do with those powders?"

"I threw them down the sink."

"What did you do with the sash weight?"

"I put it in the cellar."

"And did Ward Green come out to your house on Friday night?"

"Yes."

"What did he say?"

"He said he had come to finish the Governor."

"And what did you say?"

"I said, 'Ward, you can't do such a thing.' And then he got very upset and after a few minutes he left. But he said he was coming back again."

"Did he come back?"

"Yes."

"When was that?"

"About a week later, Saturday night. When we came back from the party, Norman and Eileen went right to bed because it was late and I was very upset to find Ward in my mother's bedroom. He was very excited, almost crazy the way he shook and shivered."

"What did he say to you?"

"He said, 'If you don't let me go through with it to-night I am going to get the pair of us.' And he had my husband's revolver that he'd gotten from the drawer and he said, 'It's either him or us.' So I grabbed him by the hand and I took him downstairs to the living room."

"When he went down with you did he have his hat and coat on?"

"No, he left them on my mother's bed."

"Did you put the weight under the pillow that night?"

"No. I put a bottle of liquor under the pillow. No weight."

"After he got downstairs did you and he have any talk?"

"We did. We talked and talked and talked. I was trying to plead with him to get the idea out of his mind. He kept getting more and more excited and I became very upset and I felt like I had to go upstairs to the bathroom."

"Did you go to the bathroom?"

"I did. And while I was in there I heard this terrific thud. I immediately opened the bathroom door and ran to the bedroom and saw Mr. Green leaning over my husband."

"Was your husband lying down or was he up?"

"My husband was lying down. Mr. Green was kneeling on his back."

"What did you do?"

"I ran in and I grabbed Mr. Green by the neck. I pulled him off and in the wrestling with me he pushed me to the floor and I fainted, and I remembered nothing until I came to again and saw my husband all piled up with blankets. I pulled the blankets off—"

She hesitated. She drew in her breath and began to weep. It was difficult at first, but she remembered how bad she had felt and how terrible Norman had looked and suddenly the crying was easier and it even relieved some of the tension she'd felt all during the questioning. She heard another series of murmurs run through the spectators, but these were different, murmurs of sympathy for her. She heard the judge clear his throat and ask the courtroom to be quiet, and she wondered if he

122

meant her. But she continued to weep, genuine tears that she really could not stop for more than a minute.

When her composure returned, the judge spoke again. "You may proceed, Mr. Whitcomb."

"Yes, sir. Mrs. Chrysler, when you came to, was Mr. Green in the room?"

"No."

"What did you do?"

"I tried to pull the blankets off my husband's head and help him. But Mr. Green came running in from the hall. 'What are you trying to do?' he screamed. 'Are you trying to ruin everything?' And he dragged me out of the room, back to my mother's room, and he said that if I didn't help him he would kill me, too. He insisted that I had to help him make it look like burglary and he ran back to the master bedroom, pulling out drawers and upsetting things, acting like a crazy man. He asked for my jewelry, saying it would look like burglary if he took it, but I wouldn't give it to him. And then he made me hide my jewelry under the mattress where the police found it. Afterward he insisted on tying me up and then, just before he left, he said I wouldn't hear from him again until I had the insurance money, and then he left."

"I see." Mr. Whitcomb paused and looked at her carefully. "Now tell me one more thing, Mrs. Chrysler. Did you, that night, strike your husband with any weight?"

"I did not."

"Did you draw a wire about his neck?"

"I did not."

"Thank you, Mrs. Chrysler. That will be all."

She did not step down immediately from the witness chair. For a moment she remained, gazing with repugnance at the man who had killed her husband. Again murmuring comment came from the spectators and she knew it was because Ward Green did not return her gaze but simply sat, head bowed like the cowardly, guilty criminal he was.

Alma slept well that night, even though Mr. Whitcomb warned her that the next day's testimony would be much more difficult. And before she went to sleep she thought a great deal about Mr. Whitcomb and the way his prematurely gray hair was combed in waves at his temples. She decided that after it was all over she would have an affair with Mr. Whitcomb, perhaps at the Waldorf or Imperial, some place nice where they could have plenty of parties and spend lots of money on the finest foods and champagnes.

The papers the next morning were jammed with columns and columns about her, repeating everything she had said in detail. She particularly liked the enormous page-one headline in the *Daily Express* which declared: WARD DID IT ALL, ALMA SAYS. Most of the editions were full of dark predictions about the tremendous court battle shaping up between Ward's attorneys and her own, the *Union-Telegram* stating that the "two former lovers will go to all lengths to lay blame for the appalling crime at one another's door."

Her cross-examination by Ward's attorneys began promptly at ten A.M. Mr. Morgan led the assault, bringing up immediately the question about the bottle of liquor she had admitted placing under the pillow for Ward. But she was ready for him, because Mr. Whitcomb had warned her that she would be asked about that and she fended him off by explaining that she had put the whisky there because Ward had asked her to.

Mr. Morgan did not seem dissatisfied with her reply. Putting his hands in his pockets, he gazed at her mildly, a partial smile on his thin lips. He was a very ugly-looking man with a twisted nose and excessively hairy, black eyebrows.

"Now then, Mrs. Chrysler," he said, "you have stated that Ward Green told you he planned to kill your husband. Did you ever warn your husband?"

"No."

"Why?"

"Because I was afraid of the disgrace if he found out about Ward and me."

"In other words, Mrs. Chrysler, if we are to believe your story we must accept the fact that you knew your husband was in danger, but you did not try in any way to help him. You did not—"

At once Mr. Whitcomb was on his feet, shouting his objection.

"Counsel is putting words in the mouth of the witness!" exclaimed Mr. Whitcomb. "He is making assumptions!"

"Objection sustained," said the judge.

It was the first of many successful objections by Mr. Whitcomb. Obviously nettled, Mr. Morgan hesitated, then began a new line of questioning.

"Tell me, Mrs. Chrysler," he said, "when you knew afterward that your husband was dead, did you cry out?"

"I was too frightened."

"Did you immediately notify any of the neighbors?"

"No, I did not."

"You simply sat there and listened to Ward Green plan a method of throwing the police off the scent?"

"I didn't know what it was all about. I was too confused."

"But you helped him make it look like burglary, did you not?"

"I had to."

Mr. Morgan smiled his dim, thin-lipped smile, turned to the jury, and then turned back to her.

"One more question, Mrs. Chrysler. When Ward Green left your house that night after the murder, did you give him another bottle of liquor to take with him on the train?"

"No, I did not."

"Thank you, Mrs. Chrysler."

Mr. Morgan then withdrew to the counsel table and did not ask any more questions. Alma sighed, a sigh too faint to be heard by the jurors or spectators, and sat back a little more comfortably in the chair.

At once the assault was continued by the chief assistant district attorney, a fortyish man named Mr. Luft, who was tall and almost as good-looking as Mr. Whitcomb, except that he was redheaded and considerably freckled.

The courtroom buzzed excitedly as Mr. Luft came forward and Alma especially noticed three women in the front row whispering among themselves as if over some savory secret.

And as soon as Mr. Luft began his questioning, she knew why the courtroom had buzzed and why the women had whispered. Because Mr. Luft had the most prying mind, the filthiest mind she had ever encountered.

"Mrs. Chrysler," he began. "did you have sexual relations with the defendant, Green, in September 1925?"

"Yes."

"That was only the third time you met him, wasn't it?"

"Yes."

"And you had sexual relations with him many times after that—in fact dozens of times?"

"Yes."

"And did your small daughter accompany you to the hotels on some occasions and wait for you in the lobby?"

"Yes."

Instantly the courtroom erupted with a roar of disapproval and one of the women down front called "Shame! Shame!" so many times the bailiff had her ejected from the building.

It was several minutes before order was restored and as Mr. Luft's filthy prying continued, the courtroom echoed again and again with noisy laughter, with unconcealed snickers and shouted insults. Again and again Mr. Whitcomb objected but was overruled.

"Is it not true, Mrs. Chrysler," said Mr. Luft, "that you have had among your acquaintances in recent years quite a few gentleman friends?"

"A few, I suppose."

"Do you know a Mr. Ralph Shrank?"

"Yes."

"Did you on August 12, 1924, have sexual relations with Mr. Shrank at the Hotel Middleton?"

"I did not."

"Do you know a Mr. Scotty McNally?"

"Yes."

"Did you on March 2, 1923 and again on March 3, and also on March 4 of that year have sexual relations with Mr. McNally at the Lafayette Hotel?"

Before she could reply, the courtroom exploded with reaction and now she realized fully for the first time why they had been there in the spectator seats day after day, packing the courtroom row after row. Scores of them with minds as filthy as Mr. Luft's, scores and scores of them waiting for moments like this, waiting to participate in this sickening carnival of prying lust directed by Mr. Luft. She felt weak, felt the blood rushing away from her brain, but she knew she mustn't faint; she must keep her wits about her through it all, the way Mr. Whitcomb said she must.

Finally the noise abated. Mr. Luft repeated the question, his voice larded with insinuation and sarcasm.

"I did not," she said, but her voice was not nearly as firm as she tried to make it.

"And do you know a Mr. James Van Der Most, a Mr. Robert Crenshaw, a Mr. George Cline, a Mr. Middleton, a Mr. Lipscomb and a dozen others? And is it not true that at varying times you had sexual relations with them all?"

"No, no, no!" she cried, but her voice was lost in the uproar, the shouts of the bailiff for order, the pounding of the judge's gavel.

It took longer, this time, to restore order and for the remainder of the session the courtroom was never really quiet. As Mr. Luft's voice went on with its sarcastic accusations, she knew she should do something to stop him, begin to weep, or shout at him, but she felt powerless and could only watch fearfully as he took up a fistful of legal papers and advanced to the jury box.

"Ladies and gentlemen," he said, and now his voice

was subdued and filled with respect and dignity. "I have here in my hand records of investigations made by the Police Department, records which prove conclusively that—"

"I object!" shouted Mr. Whitcomb. "I object!"

Once more he was overruled.

Mr. Luft raised the papers triumphantly high.

"These records," said Mr. Luft, "give the dates and places of dozens of trysts and rendezvous Alma Chrysler had with many men. And now I ask you, ladies and gentlemen, how can you accept the word of this woman when she says she had nothing to do with killing her husband? How can you accept the word of a female who was unfaithful with not just one man—as she would lead you to believe—but with over a dozen different men! Possibly as many as *eighteen* different men!"

The noise in the courtroom was so tremendous it hurt her ears. She cried out, she screamed that Mr. Luft spoke lies, but no one heard her. The judge and bailiff shouted orders, clearing the court, and then she fled to the counsel table and fell weakly against Mr. Whitcomb.

His arms were strong and very masculine as he steadied her and spoke soothing phrases close to her ear.

"It's all right, Alma," he said. "Believe me, everything's going to be all right."

chapter 14

The waiting, the waiting, the waiting. The terrible waiting was at an end. Day after day Ward Green had suffered through the hours of court procedure, the arguing, the wrangling, the outbursts. And now, this afternoon at last, they were going to let him testify, they were going to let him cast off the monstrous pressures that weighed on his conscience and soul.

With unhesitating steps he went to the witness chair. And as he sat down and saw the courtroom from this new and higher perspective, he wished the room were larger and held more people so more of them could learn and profit from the terrible things he had to tell them.

He wanted to begin his confession immediately, to purge and cleanse himself.

But it was not to be. Almost at once the delays began, the legal maneuvering by Mr. Morgan, the attorney his mother had hired for him. He knew Mr. Morgan was trying to help him, trying very hard to protect him from himself, but Mr. Morgan had no understanding, not the slightest conception, of the deep torment within him that demanded release.

Each time he tried to speak, Mr. Morgan interrupted and then the judge admonished him and he realized finally that again he must be patient, once again he must wait and wait.

The first questions were trivial and required trivial answers. When did you first meet Mrs. Chrysler? How long did you stay at the restaurant? Where did you go immediately afterward? Where is your office located? These were matters that the court had heard discussed previously by Alma and other witnesses.

"Now would you tell us," asked Mr. Morgan, "what else happened the very first night you met Mrs. Chrysler?"

"We were intimate."

"That occurred the very first time you met her, Mr. Green, and not the third time, as testified by Mrs. Chrysler?"

"That is correct. We went into the showroom at my office that night and she tried on one of the corselets, and she was badly sunburned on the shoulders, I recollect, and I had some lotion which I rubbed on her skin, and it was then that we were intimate."

He wanted to say more, he wanted to begin his long recital, the words of the long confession that had grown within him day after day, but it was not to be.

The court adjourned abruptly, because it was four o'clock, and because the judge insisted on keeping the sessions on a careful time schedule.

Frustrated, tasting the bitterness in his mouth, he waited at the counsel table with Mr. Morgan while the courtroom was cleared.

"You still mean to do it?" asked Mr. Morgan.

Ward nodded. "I must."

"You realize what it means? Possibly the difference between death or merely imprisonment?"

"I realize that," Ward said. "I realize it fully."

"Then you're a fool," said Mr. Morgan.

"Yes," said Ward. "I was a fool. And I am a fool."

The bailiff and two special officers escorted him from the courtroom. In the corridor, his mother was waiting for him as she did each day, but today there were more tear stains than usual on her deeply lined face.

She came to him at once, embracing him, her white hair touching his forehead as she kissed him gently on the cheek.

"Oh, my son, my son," she said. "Must you say those terrible things you said?"

"Yes, Mother. I must."

"You mustn't! You mustn't!"

"But, I must, Mother. I must tell the truth."

She turned to Mr. Morgan. "Can't you stop him? Can't you keep him from telling those awful things?"

"The truth may help him," Mr. Morgan said. "I only hope he doesn't say too much."

She nodded, reluctantly. "Then tell the truth, son. And I will pray that it will save you. And you must pray, son. And remember John, Chapter 8, Verse 32, '*The truth shall set ye free.*' "

The officers separated them and led him along the corridor.

"Son," she called after him, "do you have your Bible? And your prayer book?"

He nodded.

That night he did not sleep. At times he read his Bible, especially Exodus, Chapter 21. *He that smiteth a man, so that he dieth, shall surely be put to death.* More than once he thought about his wife and the terrible injury he had inflicted upon her and their daughter. He did not blame Virginia for not visiting him here or in the court-room. He was not worthy of her; he had forfeited her love. He deserved no aid from her, not even sympathy.

But mostly, through the lonely hours in his cell, he thought about what he must say the following day. And he knew there was only one course open to him, only one possible way to obtain the release which his conscience demanded.

Shortly aften ten o'clock in the morning, he was permitted to return to the stand.

Again there were procedures, delays.

But at last they let him talk.

He told of each adulterous meeting with Alma. He told of the hotel rooms, the liquor, the endless bottles of rye and gin. And as he talked he looked directly at her, looked at her where she sat at the counsel table. He met her eyes, saw the hate in them, saw her look fearfully away and grasp at the false rosary beads which she wore around her throat. With disgust he told how he could not stay away from her for more than a day at a time; he told how he was fascinated by her body, mesmerized by the animal sex of her which provoked him into doing the things that weakened him.

He sought such total degradation that he even told about the nights when he was too low in energy to be aroused by her repeated demands. He revealed her total domination of him; how she controlled his mind as well as his body; how he bought the chloroform and the sash weight; how he tested the sleeping powders for her. And as he went on his voice grew stronger and he felt as if he were talking about another person entirely, a man who was not Ward Green at all, a monstrous fornicator and drunkard, a man who did not know wrong from right and who did not care to know wrong from right.

During most of his testimony, there were no outbursts in the courtroom, no displays, few catcalls and shouted insults. He spoke the truth and they knew he was speaking the truth; they could tell the difference between his words and Alma's. During much of her testimony, Alma's voice had been stilted, hesitant, and many times her answers came too quickly, showing that she knew the questions in advance.

"And now, Mr. Green," said Mr. Morgan, "would you please state your movements on the night of March 19, starting with your arrival at the Chrysler home?"

He told it all. He left nothing out, from the objects he found under the pillow, to the moment when Alma took him by the hand and led him into the master bedroom. He told of seeing the sleeping form on the bed and of raising the sash weight high into the air.

And now for the first time he hesitated, warned by the expression in Mr. Morgan's eyes and remembering Mr. Morgan's repeated words: *"You did not strike. Remember, you did not strike. If you say you struck even one blow, you are doomed."*

Only for a moment he hesitated, and then he spoke loudly, so every person in the courtroom could hear.

"I struck him on the head! He raised up and began to holler and I believe I may have struck him again—"

There was no sound in the courtroom, not a whisper nor a rustle of clothing. He told how Norman Chrysler seized him and began choking him and how he cried out, *"Mommy! For God's sakes, help me, Mommy!"* and how she picked up the sash weight and struck her husband on the head again and again.

He did not pause.

Even when he saw Alma collapse at the counsel table, he went on with the telling of it. Even when he saw her head writhing against the table top, her fist weakly striking the surface, even then he continued with it, telling how she returned later to the bedroom and twisted the wire around her husband's neck, twisting it tightly with the golden automatic pencil from his, Ward Green's, shirt pocket.

She shrieked then, shrieked at him from her position of defeat at the counsel table.

"Stop him!" She seized the arm of her attorney and shook it wildly. "Stop him! Oh, please stop him!"

But her attorney did not rise from the counsel table. He remained beside her, shaking his head, comforting her.

Finally it was done. Finally it was told and Ward sat exhausted in the chair, breathing heavily through his mouth, unable to open his fists which had been clenched with tension in his lap throughout his long recital. But he felt no better. He felt no cleanliness. The shame and

133

the guilt weighed even heavier upon him and he knew now for certain that there could be only one release for him, one final release.

Mr. Morgan came a step closer to the witness chair. In his dark eyes there was pity and, strangely, respect.

"Thank you very much, Mr. Green." he said. "And now, if it pleases the court, I would like to make one further point. Mr. Green, will you tell us what object Mrs. Chrysler handed to you when you left her house that morning just before dawn."

"Yes, sir. A bottle of liquor."

"Did you drink it?"

"I took a taste of it."

"How did it taste?"

"Sweetish and sort of bitter."

"Thank you, Mr. Green."

Mr. Morgan walked to the exhibit table, chose a pint flask from among the numerous objects there, and strode with it to the jury box.

"Ladies and gentlemen," he said. "This, as you can see by the tag, is Exhibit No. 4. The liquor in this flask was analyzed and found to contain bichloride of mercury, an amount sufficient to kill several persons."

Mr. Morgan raised the flask higher. Reflecting the light from the chandelier overhead, its amber contents glistened with gem-like brilliance.

"Ladies and gentlemen," said Mr. Morgan, "this, I submit, is the final proof of Mrs. Chrysler's criminal mind, a mind which will still rank in years to come as one of the most savage and ruthless in criminal history. This woman, this serpent, not only drew Ward Green into her coils, compelling him to aid her in killing her husband, but she planned to destroy him as well with this bottle, leaving her free to enjoy the fruits of her crime, leaving her free to enjoy her other lovers, her other—"

It was one of the final thrills for the spectators and they greeted it with the longest, most tumultuous uproar of the trial, shrieking their condemnation of Alma

Chrysler, suppressing even the shouted objections of Mr. Whitcomb and his assistants.

What followed was anti-climactic and foregone. The closing arguments of the attorneys for both sides were lengthy and theatric, passionate and impressive, but in truth added nothing of substance to the legal proceedings.

The jury was out one hour and thirty-seven minutes.

Both defendants, Alma Chrysler and Ward Green, were found guilty of murder in the first degree.

chapter **15**

The year was 1928, the date January 12. In New York City it was a gray day, brittle with cold. In southern Georgia it was warmish, and in North Dakota and Montana a vast wind was roaring down from Canada. For most people January 12, 1928, was not much different from any other January date on the calendar.

For some, however, January 12, 1928, was a day of different character, of different routine. In the Pacific a vast search was on for two missing New Zealand fliers, Captain Hood and Lieutenant Montcrieff. In Washington, Secretary of the Navy Wilbur urged a twenty-year building program for the Navy at a cost of three billion dollars. In Forest City, Iowa, a man by the name of C. K. Johnson was fined one hundred dollars for selling cigarettes to minors. The Democrats picked Houston, Texas, for their national convention and Jack Sharkey announced that he was confident he would crush Tom Heeney during their heavyweight battle the following night at Madison Square Garden. Stocks were unsteady, the volume down.

Late in the afternoon of January 12, 1928, the final legal maneuvers on the behalf of Alma Chrysler and Ward Green ground to a halt.

The Supreme Court rejected, with finality, the request of their attorneys for a stay of execution.

At Sing Sing Prison in New York, having received no further word from the Governor's office, officials began preparing the electrocution chamber.

At exactly eleven o'clock on the night of January 12, 1928, the door opened to the cell where Alma Chrysler had spent the past eight months of her life, a period of extreme suffering, of pleading, of waiting for clemency which never arrived.

The woman who stumbled to her feet, whispering a prayer, was no longer a lovely, marcelled blonde with an apricot-smooth, Swedish complexion and clear blue eyes that welcomed love and pleasure. The figure was no longer erect and narrow-waisted, with seductive movements of hip and breast.

The woman who was led along the twisting prison corridor had gaunt white cheeks. She appeared to be forty-five or possibly fifty years of age. Her hair was long, stringy and decidedly gray. Her jaw was prominent and bony, her eyes glazed with fear. Her shoulders and neck were bent forward as if with some crippling disease, and she was garbed in a shapeless black prison garment, heavy black cotton stockings and rough shoes.

Two matrons half-carried her, half-dragged her into the death chamber.

She was too filled with terror to hear the gasps of astonishment which came from the assembled reporters when they first saw her.

Mercifully, as the matrons strapped her into the chair, she did not hear the whispered comment of the correspondent in the second row who stood on tiptoe to get a better view.

"My God!" he said. "They've got the wrong woman!"

At eleven-ten, Ward Green entered the death chamber. He needed no assistance as he walked with firm steps to the chair. He did not surrender his Bible to the guards until the straps were fixed and tight. And then, in a low, calm voice he thanked them for letting him keep the book with him until his final seconds.

At eleven-thirty P.M. on January 12, 1928, Alma Chrysler and Ward Green lay together for the last time. They lay side by side on separate wheeled stretchers in the prison mortuary room.

Their eyes were closed and their hands did not touch.

THE END